I'LL TAKE YOUR MAN

WRITTEN & STORY

BY

CHARLIE BASSETT JR.

This is a work of fiction. Names, places, and incidents are products of the author's imagination or are used fictitiously. Any resemblance to actual events or locales or persons, living or dead, is entirely coincidental.

Ta-La-Vue Publishing
P.O. Box 942
Pottstown, Pa 19464

ISBN: 978-0-9797521-0-0
Written and storied by Charlie Bassett Jr.
Type setting by George Murrille
Editing by V.R. Editing
Cover by Tony Lew
Model: Joanne Singletary
Printing: Malloy, Inc.

Printed in the United States of America.

DEDICATION

This book is dedicated to my struggle and to everyone who ever lifted a finger to help!

And to every woman who had to deal with the other woman in her man's life.

ACKNOWLEDGEMENTS

All praise is due to the creator, for the mercy that is bestowed upon us.

I thank my family for their emotional and financial support through the years: Evelyn, Katrina, Sherri, Julius, Cryus, Unisha Jefferson, the Nieces & Nephews, Keith, Marquetta, Champ, and Roosevelt.

Special thanks to Vern who was an integral part in the writing of this book.

Thanks to supportive friends: Hasan, Karim, Sunni Ali, Basir, Rell, J-Moe, Black, Kevin, Kabir, Karl, Dre, Joe, Big Joann & Little Joann, Malik, Robin, Dave, Patty, Mr. Ross, and Rob.

For all those whose names evade me at this moment and for all those who will lend a hand after this book is printed. And for those who may support me in future endeavors.

And last, but certainly not least, to you Saibah my love, support, motivator and inspiration. A special thanks to you for inspiring me to stop toying with my talent and make something happen! To this I'm grateful.

CHAPTER 1

Thirty-year-old Ashley Gray strolled down the radio station corridor towards her studio. Ashley, the ultimate head turner, walked with the illustration of a Hollywood starlet without the makeup.

From her skin tone, she looked like she was dipped in cinnamon. Her face was void of flaws. She had puffy pink kissable lips, her legs were long and lean, and her thighs were highlighted by a short miniskirt two inches away from exposing her crotch area.

She sported three inch heels that exhibited the roundness of her calves. Her jet black mane was tied in a ponytail and bounced on her back with each step she took. Her ass, which was her pride and joy, was ideal for the advertisement of hip-cut jeans.

Five years earlier when Ashley first started working at the radio station, there were rumors that she had breast and ass implants, but they were just rumors, started by a female hater. Ashley was born with the physical attributes that many women were currently paying for.

When Ashley arrived at her studio, there was a 22-year-old female intern waiting outside the door with a cup of coffee in hand. Ashley took the coffee and mouthed the words thank you, insincerely. What a bitch, the intern thought as she walked away.

Ashley settled into her chair and pulled her microphone close to her. Ashley was a radio personality. Not just any chick with a mic, she was The Chick with a mic. Her radio show was number one in the region with subjects ranging from teenage pregnancy to foursomes. Quite frankly, nothing was off limits.

Haters, as well as Ashley's fans, tuned in daily to hear what outlandish thing Ashley would say next. When it came to liking or disliking Ashley Gray, no one straddled the fence, you either loved or hated her. However you chose, she could care less.

As Ashley's popularity grew, so did her opposition. There was always some sort of protest outside the station. But all that the hoopla garnered was off the chart ratings which translated to more money in Ashley's pockets.

For the past week Ashley had the airways blazing with her controversial topic: Why do men chase women? Look at this ass! Ashley made it clear that the ass she was referring to was her very own.

When Ashley began discussing this topic with her audience she took the gloves off, she opened up her black-book and let it all hang out.

She basically brought her bedroom romps to her show. Airing her dirty laundry to over a million listeners was an afterthought.

Now she was two minutes away from doing it all again. Ashley let the world know that her preferred man was one who was married or had a girlfriend. Simply put, they were convenient for her lifestyle.

Ten seconds before going on the air, Ashley started the count down in her head then clicked on her microphone.

"Hey." Ashley spoke into the microphone in a low and sexual voice. "Hey" was her routine opening.

"Why do men chase women? Somebody holler at me," Ashley said in her regular voice plugging in her first caller.

"Hey Ash," A male caller said trying to sound overly masculine.

"What's up big guy, why do men chase women?"

"Well I saw your pretty ass the other night and those legs of yours would look good on my shoulders."

"I don't know about that. Do you have a girl or are you married?"

"No, I'm single and available," The caller said boastfully.

"Well you blew it buddy. I'm only into men who are taken. I need a guy I can send back to his wife when I'm done, no strings attached."

Ashley plugged a female caller in.

"You are a dirty bitch! You're going to hell!"

"Well sweetheart there'll be plenty of men there with me. Maybe yours, stop hating." Ashley chuckled then clicked the caller off.

"Before I go to a commercial, I want to key y'all in to my latest relationship. I've been dating this guy for a couple of months, let's call him Bob, and yes he's married. His wife is 40ish and works at a hospital, she's a doctor or a nurse. They have a kid about 3-years-old, a boy or a girl, whatever, who cares. When the wife found out Bob was cheating, she kicked him out of the house, now he's sleeping on a friend's couch."

Ashley plugged in a female caller.

"Don't you have any feelings for Bob's wife?"

"Yes, that's why I'm being a good sport by dumping his lazy ass and sending him home. I hear Bob is all torn up these days, maybe his wife can put him back together."

CHAPTER 2

Boiling with anger, beads of sweat freckled Tasha's nose and cheeks as she turned off the radio. She must be a freak for pain, she thought, because for the life of her she couldn't figure out why she tortured herself by listening to Ashley's radio show.

She sat on the couch and wiped away tears that were slowly tracking down her cheek. She snatched a Kleenex tissue from the box, blew her nose, then tossed the tissue in the wastebasket filled with snotty tissues.

Tasha stared at the radio as if it would come back to life at any moment blaring Ashley's taunting voice. Why do men chase women? Look at this ass! Ashley's words echoed in Tasha's mind, bringing on a headache. She tried to chase the words away by yelling, "Fuck your ass Ashley!" It didn't work.

Tasha's 3-year-old daughter, who was sitting on the floor playing with her doll, looked quickly around the room for the person who caused her mother's rage. Seeing no one, the child looked up at Tasha strangely.

Tasha had every right to be angry. Three days earlier she discovered that her husband Bruce had been cheating again so she kicked him out of the house.

What made matters worse, Bruce was laid off from work and living off Tasha who was working overtime and keeping him garbed in the latest fashion. Tasha hated that she was dick-whipped, but this time she was determined to stand tough, at least for a while.

Although Bruce never mentioned the name of his latest paramour, it was easy for Tasha to conclude that the guilty party was Ashley for several reasons.

Bruce always cheated with women who had money, because he had none to give. And the name Ashley used for her guy, Bob, was close to the name Bruce. And there were other similarities, for instance, Tasha was 40-years-old and worked at a hospital as a nurse, and they have a 3-year-old daughter, not a boy, whatever, as Ashley had put it.

That was enough for Tasha to charge Ashley as the bitch who ruined her family.

Tasha had never saw Ashley before, but assumed like all the other women who Bruce had flings with, Ashley was probably beautiful. Complimenting the other woman left Tasha even angrier and feeling stupid.

She stood up and walked in front of the full-length mirror and stared, not so kindly, at her reflection. She was clad in baggy nondescript pajamas. Ashley's probably dressed to kill, Tasha thought enviously.

Tasha wasn't the hot nurse you saw on television or in the movies. She was average, hair cropped short because it was easier to manage. She had dark rings around her eyes from late nights and early mornings of helping doctors save lives.

She wondered if Ashley had ever helped save a life, and figured the whore probably didn't, too busy ruining them.

Tasha stood 5'1" and 157 pounds, mostly baby fat she had neither the time nor energy to lose. Tasha patted her chubby thighs. She hated her short legs. Ashley's legs are probably long and slender, she guessed correctly.

As Tasha tore herself down in the mirror, her daughter walked over and patted Tasha's thigh and said, "Mommy your leg is fat."

That was the last straw. Tasha put her daughter to

bed. She then changed into a cotton sweat-suit and slid on her Nike track sneakers.

Looking psyched up, Tasha marched back to the living room and stood before the full-length mirror determined to do at least thirty minutes of aerobics.

Tasha began her workout by doing fifteen jumping jacks. Unfortunately, that was all she could muster before fizzling out. Three minutes later, Tasha laid in her bed sobbing. She had one thought in her head, fuck your stinking ass Ashley!

CHAPTER 3

Twenty two-year-old D'neen was a cute and shy college student who was majoring in communications. Two months earlier she married her high school sweetheart, Charles, and together they moved from their small hometown in the Midwest to the city.

Of all the houses in the city that were for rent or sale, D'neen and Charles decided on a beautiful three-bedroom house with a garage that just happened to be next door to Ashley's.

When Ashley learned that her new neighbor was studying communications, she got D'neen on as an intern at the radio station.

And of course, Ashley did take notice of Charles, who was medium height, dark, lean and fit, and extremely handsome. She was prepared to make a move on him, but at the last minute, she decided to behave, at least for the time being.

Although D'neen and Ashley were neighbors and worked at the same radio station, they had little interaction. At work D'neen congregated with the other interns learning the business. As for Ashley, she strutted around the station with her head in the clouds, usually in the company of men, while the women watched with smiles on their faces masking their jealousy.

D'neen learned quickly that because of Ashley's clout, none of the women at the station dared to say anything negative about Ashley in her presence. Ashley made it known verbally, "I have no problem with getting a bitch fired!"

On a pleasant summer evening, Ashley and D'neen's divide came to an end. D'neen was leaving from work, walking through the parking lot towards her car when Ashley approached her from behind.

"Hey Baby Doll, can I get a ride?" Ashley asked smiling.

During their ride home, Ashley made D'neen nervous by constantly staring and smiling at her. Ashley was the type of person who thrived on fucking with people's heads and when she realized that D'neen was uncomfortable by her staring, she turned up the heat.

As D'neen drove, she wished she had worn pants instead of the skirt that was hiked up along her thighs. Ashley boldly gazed at D'neen's thighs, then into the shy girl's face, then back to her thighs. D'neen wanted to pull her skirt closer to her knees but didn't.

Ashley's flirtatious manner gave D'neen a jolt that caused her to take her eyes off the road for a second which almost resulted in an accident.

Although D'neen had dismissed the rumors about Ashley's promiscuous lifestyle, because she never saw any men or women coming or going from Ashley's house, she was now beginning to think twice about her earlier assessment based on Ashley's current behavior.

Bracing herself for a sexual proposition from Ashley, D'neen contemplated several pleasant rejection lines to let her feisty neighbor down easy.

The last thing she wanted to do was piss off Ashley who had been so nice to her. D'neen finally drove to their neighborhood, a quiet suburban section of the city. She turned the car on to Kelly Street, their block.

D'neen pulled the car to the curb stopping in front of her house. With the back of her hand, Ashley touched

D'neen's cheek lightly.

"Thanks for the ride Baby Doll."

D'neen thought about asking Ashley not to call her Baby Doll, but decided against it, figuring it wasn't a big deal.

As D'neen opened her door to exit, Ashley reached out and placed her hand on D'neen's shoulder. D'neen tensed up and cut her eye sharply at Ashley.

"Listen Baby Doll, why don't you join me --"

Before Ashley could finish, D'neen spun around in her seat facing Ashley.

"I'm not into women, I'm married," D'neen expounded sternly, but also apologetically.

"What's on your mind Baby Doll, I was going to ask you if you wanted to co-host my show tomorrow?" Ashley pretended to be shocked by D'neen's reaction.

Although she dallied with D'neen's head, Ashley did have intentions on inviting D'neen to do the show.

"I'm so sorry." D'neen looked embarrassed. She pondered a moment, "Sure, I would love to do your show."

"Good, you can bring some morals to the show."

They laughed then exited the car and walked towards their respective houses. Ashley stopped and turned back towards D'neen.

"Baby Doll!" Ashley called out.

D'neen stopped and turned towards Ashley.

"Tell Charles I asked about him," Ashley said nonchalantly.

Without waiting for a response, Ashley entered her house and laughed out loud about toying with D'neen.

D'neen walked in her own house perplexed by Ashley's remark. D'neen may have been a square, but she wasn't that slow to give Charles Ashley's message.

CHAPTER 4

From across the street, Katrina peered out her window watching Ashley and D'neen as they exited D'neen's car. Katrina's attention was focused solely on Ashley who she despised.

As far as an opinion of D'neen, Katrina only had two brief encounters with her and found the girl quiet, but likable. However, she was now viewing D'neen in two different lights.

She figured the girl was either an undercover whore or very naïve to be palling around with Ashley. Katrina gave D'neen the benefit of the doubt and believed the latter.

In either case, D'neen was soon to learn the hard way for taking up company with a snake like Ashley, Katrina thought.

Katrina was a 33-year-old house wife. Her life was one of boredom and her marriage was hanging by a thread with a five pound weight on it, courtesy of Ashley.

The trouble between Ashley and Katrina commenced five years earlier. Katrina was living on Kelly Street with her boyfriend Lewis when Ashley moved on the block.

The two women became friends immediately: partying into the early morning hours, lounging at each other's houses puffing weed, and going clothes shopping.

But the wedge in the relationship was lodged when Katrina married Lewis and stopping partying. Feeling snubbed, Ashley became jealous.

Before Lewis became the successful entrepreneur he was today, he worked at the radio station. As a favor to Katrina, Lewis had gotten Ashley a job there.

Ashley repaid Lewis with the best blow job of his life. Katrina's reward was catching them in the act. The sight of Ashley gobbling down on her husband had a lasting affect on Katrina in more ways than one.

For months Lewis cried, pleaded, and begged for a second chance. Finally, against her better judgment, Katrina accepted him back. Unfortunately, their marriage would never be the same.

Katrina, who rivaled Ashley in beauty, lost self-esteem and desire to dress up, and her ability to trust, among other things.

Seeing Ashley everyday didn't help matters. Initially Katrina wanted to move, but something changed in her. She became defiant and decided that she wasn't going to let Ashley Gray run her away from her home.

After spying on D'neen and Ashley, Katrina took a shower, then crawled in bed with a romance novel.

Ten minutes later, Lewis entered. He and Katrina greeted each other without breaking their stride from what they were doing, Katrina reading, and Lewis undressing.

Lewis was medium height, slender, and unassuming. Most women wouldn't give him a second look unless they knew of the balance in his savings account.

Lewis placed his cell phone on the dresser then went into the bathroom and showered. His get-out-of-the-house plan was already in effect.

Lewis had told his business partner to call his phone, ten minutes after Lewis got home. He would be in the shower, so Katrina would answer the phone. The partner would sound disturbed and tell Katrina to have Lewis call him A.S.A.P. Lewis knew the plan was old and cheesy, but it would work.

Ten minutes later, Lewis entered the bedroom and things went as planned.

"Kevin called and said it was an emergency."

Lewis grabbed his phone and called Kevin.

"Yo, what's up?" Lewis said inquisitively. He then listened to Kevin, who jokingly warned him against cheating on Katrina.

Lewis caught Katrina occasionally watching him.

"That's impossible," Lewis said, hyping up his concern for the fictitious problem.

Lewis hung up the phone and started getting dressed.

"What happened?" Katrina asked.

"Kevin -- this money, I have to take care of this or it won't get done."

Katrina wasn't sure if it was a legitimate emergency or not, but since Lewis was paying the bills and putting money in her pocket, she couldn't doubt it when he said he had to take care of business.

Lewis' type of work demanded late hours, trips out of town, and getting up in the middle of the night to fix a problem. Knowing that Katrina understood his occupation, Lewis used it to his advantage.

***

Five minutes after leaving his house, Lewis was naked in Ashley's bed with his head between her legs. Ashley moaned with stimulated pleasure, along with the satisfaction that Katrina's husband was at her beckon call.

Ashley didn't really like Lewis, she fucked him for two reasons. The first was something trivial. Ashley believed by having sex with Lewis she had one up on Katrina, and signified it by smirking whenever they crossed paths.

The second reason, Lewis' tongue was incredible, touching places that made Ashley tremble so much so that, she wanted to slap him every time she had an orgasm.

Even with the pleasure Ashley received from Lewis

she wanted to break off the affair, but she kept him on call until someone better or of equal talents came along to fill the vacuum.

After their intercourse, Lewis took a shower. As he washed he felt pretty slick. He had just had sex with one of the hottest women in the city, and he could go home smelling freshly bathed without Katrina grilling him with twenty questions.

But in the back of his mind Lewis knew he had to be careful. Although he cheated, he was very much afraid of Katrina. He remembered her promise to cut off his manhood if he ever hurt her again, and he believed that she would do it.

Lewis dried with a towel, dressed, then kissed Ashley goodnight and left out the backdoor. His fling with Ashley had taken twenty minutes, so he drove around for ten minutes before returning home.

***

Next door at D'neen's house, she rolled off of her husband Charles' body. Both of them breathing heavily and drenched in sweat.

"Ashley wants me to do her show tomorrow."

Charles frowned in the dark. "What?"

D'neen knew that Charles didn't approve of Ashley's show or how she portrayed herself.

"I'm going to speak on the virtues of marriage."

Charles thought about it for a moment, "Ashley isn't cool."

"She is. She just gets a bad rap because she's conceited and handles her business."

Charles may have been from the same small town as D'neen, but he wasn't as green as she. Charles was about to tell D'neen to stay away from Ashley but decided against it.

"When you go on the air tomorrow make sure you tell the world how you shake when I make you cum."

D'neen laughed and pinched his nipple. Charles rubbed D'neen's inner thigh with his open hand. She responded immediately by climbing on top of him for the second time that night.

CHAPTER 5

D'neen sat nervously in Ashley' studio staring at the microphone inches away from her face. In a matter of moments her voice will hit the airways echoing in the homes of over a million listeners.

Ashley leaned over and cupped D'neen's face in her hands then whispered, "Relax."

D'neen smiled, nodding her head affirmatively, then took a deep breath. D'neen's eyes were wide, filled with excitement and anticipation.

Ashley sat in her chair and adjusted her microphone closer to her. She hit a switch on the console, then in traditional fashion she said, "Hey" into the microphone.

D'neen smiled at Ashley who returned the gesture with a wink. D'neen thought, this woman has her act together.

"I have in the studio a very special friend, my girl D'neen, A.K.A Baby Doll. She's an intern here at the station, she's beautiful, and a newlywed."

D'neen didn't immediately respond. She was wondering why Ashley would lie by saying she was also known as Baby Doll. Ashley was gesturing with her hands for D'neen to say something.

"Hello," D'neen finally said in a nervous voice.

"D'neen's a little shy, maybe we should've given her a drink to loosen her up. I hear that works well for virgins."

D'neen giggled like a Geisha girl. She remembered that helped relax her with Charles when he popped her cherry.

"Let's get straight to the point. D'neen in your opinion, why do men chase women? Is it the animal instinct in them?"

"Quite frankly, that's generalizing. I don't believe all men chase women."

Ashley was surprised by D'neen's forwardness.

"And what planet is this you lived on before coming to earth?" Ashley asked.

D'neen took offense, but masked it with a smile.

"Well, if I thought that all men were dogs as you suggest that they are, I wouldn't have married my husband," D'neen offered jauntily.

"Fair enough. But I've been keeping score and it seems to me that men cheat quite frequently at one time or another."

"Maybe the men you allow into your intimacy have issues with commitment," D'neen said sympathetically.

No this little country bitch is not trying to put me on blast on my own show, Ashley said to herself.

"You have women out there who encourage the chase, and that says a lot about her character," D'neen added.

Is this bitch throwing verbal jabs at me, Ashley was wondering. At that moment, Ashley vowed that she was going to make D'neen eat her words.

"So how's the marriage?"

The question caught D'neen off guard.

"Charles and I are well."

"Well? Not terrific or great?" Ashley asked searching for an opening.

"My marriage is excellent, I have no complaints."

"Does Charles?" Ashley joked with a smile.

This time D'neen couldn't mask her dismay, but she turned away from Ashley refusing to give Ashley the pleasure of seeing her anger.

"Does Charles like the chase?" Ashley reiterated raising her eyebrows at D'neen.

"I don't believe Charles would ever be unfaithful. When a couple has a healthy sex life and they're honest with each other among other things, there is no reason to stray. Besides, why would Charles want to cheat, look at this ass," D'neen said sarcastically.

Ashley smiled and thought, I can't wait to crush this little bitch. Ashley leaned over and patted D'neen on the side of her butt.

"I must admit guys, Baby Doll is holding."

"For Charles only," D'neen interjected.

Ashley was really becoming agitated but hid it with a smile.

"D'neen do you know the signs of a cheating husband?"

D'neen was irked by the question and let it show.

"I guess a woman would recognize a change in her man."

"Not so," Ashley said jumping in. "I've had several men whose wives and girlfriends were in the dark to our affairs. Do you think a woman who's as clever as I could be with your husband and keep you in the dark?" Ashley said challenging.

D'neen glared at Ashley. Ashley laughed knowing she struck a nerve.

"Hold on Baby Doll, I'm not talking about me per-se."

After a few more exchanges of verbal jabs, the show ended. Ashley stood up and stretched, then embraced D'neen, who returned the hug but didn't know exactly how she felt about Ashley at the moment.

"That was interesting. I thought you were shy?"

"I guess this was my coming out party."

"I know things got a little testy, but it was all a part

of the show." Ashley spoke sincerely, but harbored insincere feelings in her heart towards D'neen.

D'neen decided that Ashley's comments were about ratings so she wasn't going to hold a grudge.

"A friend of mine is getting married Friday. Important people are going to be there, I want you and Charles to come with me."

"I don't know." D'neen figured Charles would decline.

"Y'all are coming with me, that's final, tell Charles."

CHAPTER 6

Tasha was walking down the hospital hallway when she got a page to come to the nurse's station. As she turned the corner, she looked towards the station and saw Bruce standing there with his back to her talking to a nurse seated at the station.

Tasha stopped and debated with the decision whether to advance or turn around and head to where she came from. She reluctantly decided to confront Bruce.

Bruce was a pretty boy—metro sexual from his hair to his toes. Although it drove Tasha crazy when he took an hour-plus to bathe, groom, and dress, nevertheless, she liked the fact that her man took care in looking his best.

As Tasha approached Bruce, the nurse he was speaking to pointed past him towards Tasha. Bruce turned around facing Tasha with a smile on his face and a rose in his hand. He extended his arm, offering the rose. Tasha looked at the rose, sighed, and folded her arms across her chest.

"I just wanted to see how you were doing," Bruce said genuinely.

"I'm maintaining."

"How's my daughter?"

"She's maintaining," Tasha said sharply.

Bruce was about to challenge Tasha's attitude but settled on another approach, he just stared at her. Tasha held his gaze for a moment then averted her eyes. She knew what he was trying to do. Looking into his eyes was hypnotic, he could stare her out of her panties. But Tasha was not ready to forgive.

"You saw how I'm doing, now what?"

"I'm sorry baby."

Tasha didn't respond. Bruce took a step towards her, she took a step back. She couldn't let him touch her. Bruce's hand upon her bare skin had the power to manipulate her sense of reasoning. Tasha hated that she was dick whipped.

"I have to get back to work."

"Okay…I just wanted to see you, I was going to stop by the house but I figured that wouldn't be a good idea right now."

"You're absolutely right," Tasha said with attitude.

Bruce's eyes left Tasha and looked past her, she turned to see what had grabbed his attention. It was a beautiful woman. The woman walked past them swaying her hips, but not before cutting her eye at Bruce, checking him out with a glance.

It took all of Bruce's strength to resist turning around to check out the women from behind. Tasha looked jealous and annoyed, because she knew he wanted to look.

"Okay, I'm going to let you get back to work."

"Where are you headed?" Tasha asked.

Tasha didn't care where Bruce was headed. She only asked the question to keep him from chasing behind the woman.

"Uh, no where particular. Why you ask?"

"I don't know. I'll tell our daughter you said hello."

"When can I stop by to see her?"

"I'll give you a call, bye," Tasha said turning to leave.

"Tasha, wait a second please."

Tasha turned to face Bruce. He looked abashed as he managed a half-hearted smile.

"Damn, I hate this-- baby can I hold twenty dollars?"

Tasha rolled her eyes, pondered a moment, then reached in her pocket and pulled out a twenty dollar bill and handed it to him. The nurse who was seated at the station and watching shook her head disapprovingly.

"Thanks," Bruce said, leaning to kiss Tasha.

She avoided the kiss by stepping back from him. Bruce nodded his head understandingly.

"I know you might believe otherwise, but I love you baby."

Bruce then walked down the hallway towards the exit. Tasha walked over to the nurse's station, the nurse there looked at Tasha pitifully.

"I guess he didn't get a job yet?" The nurse said, asking and answering her own question.

"He's looking?" Tasha said forcing smile.

The nurse knew Tasha was defending Bruce so she changed the subject.

"I'm going to a wedding Friday, you want to come?" The nurse asked invitingly.

"Who's throwing their lives away?" Tasha responded with a smile.

***

Katrina walked out of her kitchen into the living room, trailed by Lewis.

"You know I don't do churches," Katrina said flopping down on the sofa eating from a pint of strawberry ice cream, her favorite.

"Their house is huge. Everything's going to be outside in the front yard, the wedding and reception. It's about time you got out the house, don't say no," Lewis said pleadingly.

"Who gets married on a Friday?" Katrina asked.

"My friend does."

"Why haven't I ever heard of this friend?"

"He and I just started doing business together."

"Will anybody I know be there?" Katrina asked offhandedly.

"I don't know, I don't think so."

If it was any other event, Lewis wouldn't have asked Katrina to accompany him. But he figured attending a wedding might spark Katrina's matrimonial spirits and re-energized his failing marriage.

Yes, Lewis was a lowdown, rotten cheater. But he knew what he had in Katrina, she was faithful, honest, and trustworthy and he loved her. So, at that point, he believed his marriage was worth saving.

CHAPTER 7

It was a lovely Friday afternoon. The front yard to a beautiful home in the backdrop was teeming with wedding guests who were dancing, mingling, and sitting around enjoying the festive atmosphere.

The bride and groom had married twenty minutes earlier, now they were gazing into each other eyes as they danced under the watchful eyes of their guest.

Tasha sat alone at a table, reminiscing about her own wedding. She remembered thinking there was nothing in the world that could come between her and Bruce. She wondered if the newlyweds in front of her felt the same way she had once felt about her own marriage.

Of course they do she concluded, because every couple on their wedding day believes their marriage will last forever.

On the other side of the yard, Katrina stood alone eyeing Lewis who was conversing with two other men. Knowing Lewis, she figured the men were discussing business, and she was right because Lewis never missed a chance to make a dollar.

Bored with standing alone, Katrina walked through the yard looking for a seat and friendly face to socialize with. She believed she found both in the woman who was sitting alone at a table. The woman was Tasha. Katrina walked over to her.

"Hi, you mind if I sit here?" Katrina asked politely.

"No," Tasha said returning Katrina's smile.

For a moment the two women were silent as they watched the bride and groom dance.

"They're an attractive couple," Tasha complemented.

"It takes more than good looks to hold a marriage together," Katrina responded.

They both nodded in agreement. Tasha extended her hand toward Katrina who shook it.

"I'm Tasha."

"Katrina."

"I love your bracelet," Tasha said admiringly.

She noticed Katrina's bracelets when they shook hands. Katrina twirled them a couple of times.

"I made them myself. I can make you some if you like?"

From that, Tasha and Katrina exchanged phone numbers and stories of their troubled marriages.

"Do you think they're going to make it?" Tasha asked still watching the newlyweds while they danced as if they were the only people on earth.

"Yeah, if he doesn't sleep around," Katrina said jokingly.

Tasha and Katrina laughed, and then went silent as they checked out the guests and what they were doing. That's when Tasha saw Bruce walking towards them.

"That's my husband, what's he doing here?" Tasha said talking to herself but speaking out loud.

Bruce walked over to the table.

"Hey baby," Bruce said as he leaned to kiss Tasha.

Tasha gave him a look that halted his efforts. Katrina smiled. At that moment she knew that she and Tasha would become good friends.

"What are you doing here?" Tasha asked sternly.

"The groom is a friend of mine."

"Well, I'm talking to my friend right now, could you give us some privacy?"

Bruce looked at Katrina then back to Tasha. He wanted to grill her for embarrassing him but he decided to bite the bullet and smile.

"Okay, but I want to dance with you before you leave."

Tasha laughed. Bruce chuckled trying to play Tasha's laugh off. Without saying another word he walked away to the far end of the yard and stopped there.

Moments later there was commotion and murmuring among the guests. Tasha and Katrina both stood to see what had caused the stirring. It was a 2008 Dark Sapphire Bentley Continental Flying Spur that had pulled in front of the yard with the music blaring.

The music from the car was killed, the door opened, Ashley emerged, followed by D'neen and Charles.

They walked into the yard with all eyes upon them. But the attention was really on Ashley who looked elegant in a white gown with the back out.

"Leave it up to Ashley Gray to up-stage the bride," said one guest to another.

"Who is she?" Tasha asked jovially.

Katrina didn't respond. Tasha, who was gaping at Ashley, didn't see the fire in Katrina's eyes.

"Is she a model or an actress?" Tasha was at this time speaking to herself.

"She's a whore who moonlights as a radio personality. I'm sure you heard of her, Ashley Gray. She's the bitch that fucked my husband."

Tasha was stunned speechless as her smiled withered away. She thought Ashley was probably pretty, but not this gorgeous. At that moment Tasha lost what was left of her fragile self-esteem.

After a moment of regrouping, the life seeped back into Tasha's body.

"I think she's the woman who Bruce had an affair with," Tasha said just above a whisper.

Katrina wasn't surprised, she just shook her head, "Welcome to the club. You should go over there and kick her ass," Katrina suggested to Tasha's surprise.

Tasha wasn't going to confront Ashley in front of all the guest and she proved it by sitting down. Katrina also sat down. However, Tasha was deciding how best to approach the situation.

As Tasha pondered in silence, she and Katrina both spied on their husbands, watching for anything that would suggest that the husbands took the slightest interest in Ashley. Both men made it their business to avoid looking in Ashley's direction, they knew their wives were watching.

Ashley moved through the yard as if she was floating three inches from the ground. D'neen and Charles followed her like two puppies.

Ashley introduced them to one person after the next. Ashley saw both Bruce and Lewis in attendance, but was unfazed by their presence. She simply paid them both no attention.

"I wanna dance, come on Charles," Ashley said out of the blue.

Charles and D'neen were both caught off guard.

"I don't --" Charles mumbled.

Ashley interrupted, "Please don't make me dance alone. D'neen, it's okay isn't it?"

"Yeah, it's okay with me," D'neen said, not wanting to come off as insecure.

Before Charles could object, Ashley had pulled him into the dance. D'neen found herself standing alone feeling foolish, so she walked over toward the table area where she saw Katrina and Tasha sitting.

"Hi Katrina."

"Hello D'neen -- D'neen this is Tasha."

The two women exchanged their greetings as D'neen took a seat at the table and watched Ashley and Charles.

As Charles and Ashley danced, there was a handsome

man with salt and pepper hair standing a few yards behind Charles and staring at Ashley. She held his gaze as they smiled at each other. Ashley guessed he was in his late forties.

Over at the table, Katrina shook her head at D'neen. "Why are you over here and that snake is over there with your man?"

"They're only dancing," D'neen responded trying to sound unconcerned.

As Katrina and D'neen chitchatted, Tasha thought she saw eye contact made between Bruce and Ashley.

"If I was you I would go get my man," Katrina warned, as Ashley moved closer to Charles as they danced. That was enough for D'neen. She rushed over to Charles and Ashley.

Tasha marched over to Bruce. He saw her coming, he also saw the anger on her face. Bruce was wondering how Tasha found out it was Ashley that he had been seeing, if that was her beef. Before he knew what hit him, Tasha slapped him hard across the face.

The music stopped on cue and the guests turned to watch. Ashley, who was now conversing with the handsome man who have been eyeing her while she danced, watched also.

"That's the bitch you're fucking?" Tasha yelled.

"Are you drunk or something, what are you talking--"

Before Bruce could finish his sentence Tasha slapped him.

"Don't put your hands on me again!"

Tasha swung again, but this time Bruce grasped her wrist in mid-air, at which time the groom walked over.

"Bruce this is my wedding, I can't have this here."

Tasha looked around and saw everyone watching her and was embarrassed. She apologized to the groom then walked through the yard towards her car, followed by Bruce.

Katrina walked over to Lewis.

"We're leaving," Katrina said in gruff voice.

As Katrina turned to leave she bumped into the handsome man walking with Ashley. His drink spilled onto Katrina's dress. Ashley placed her hand over her mouth to muzzle her laugh. But Katrina could see the laughter in Ashley's eyes.

"I'm so sorry," the man said apologetically.

Katrina didn't respond, she just glared at Ashley. Then without warning, she charged Ashley. But Ashley was fast, almost expecting this kind of reaction from Katrina.

Ashley weaved pass Katrina, by that time several guests restrained Katrina who was ranting and raving.

Ashley strutted to her car and sped away. The handsome man, who was oblivious to the undertone surrounding the spilled drink, jogged to his car and followed her.

Ten minutes later Charles was pissed as he and D'neen hopped in a cab and headed home.

CHAPTER 8

Lewis entered his house followed by Katrina, who was furious. She slammed the front door behind her.

"You knew that bitch was going to be there," Katrina said pointing a finger in Lewis' face.

"How could I know, I don't communicate with her," Lewis grumbled as he walked away from Katrina to the other side of the room.

Katrina looked at her dress and shook her head, "That bitch deliberately spilled that drink on my dress," Katrina complained loudly to herself.

"Ashley didn't do it, the guy she was talking to spilled the drink."

Katrina was jarred as she stared at Lewis in disbelief. No he didn't just defend that bitch, she thought.

From the enraged look on Katrina's face, Lewis knew he had made a mistake. He knew he had to act fast before things got ugly.

"I know what you're thinking. I wasn't defending Ashley, I was only pointing out the truth," Lewis said passively as he moved toward Katrina.

He placed his hands on Katrina's waist and pulled her close, gazing into her eyes.

"The last thing I want to do is hurt your feelings. Let's just put this day behind us. I'm tired and I know you're probably tired as well so let's not fight, okay?" Lewis said softly.

Katrina pondered for a moment, allowing the anger in her face to dissipate. Lewis was glad to see her simmering down.

"You're right," Katrina said smiling.

"Good."

Lewis smiled back at Katrina and kissed her on the forehead then walked upstairs.

Later that night Katrina stood at the side of the bed watching Lewis as he slept soundly. Katrina had her arms to her side and in her left hand was a box-cutter.

She crawled in bed next to Lewis and began massaging his penis with her right hand. Lewis came to life in more ways than one. Katrina leaned over and stuck her tongue in his mouth, snaking her tongue along his. As they kissed, she continued to massage him then slowly leveled the box-cutter blade to Lewis' neck.

Feeling the metal against his neck, Lewis' body stiffened in fear, except for his hard-on. It shriveled in Katrina's hand. Lewis swallowed hard. The movement of his Adam's apple against the blade almost drew blood.

"If you ever defend that bitch again I will hurt you," Katrina said in a frightening voice. A voice Lewis had never heard before.

"Do we have an understanding?"

"Yes," Lewis replied meekly.

Katrina stood up and withdrew the blade back into the case.

"I'm going to finish sewing. Go back to sleep baby. I really didn't want to wake you up, but I had to get that off my chest you understand," Katrina said in her regular voice, then walked out of the room as if nothing had transpired.

For minutes Lewis laid in bed traumatized. When he regained his composure, he wanted to go and beat Katrina's ass, but he wasn't sure he could get away with it. So he laid there thinking, I have to get away from this crazy bitch.

***

Across the street, Charles' head was buried between D'neen's legs. Her body shook like a virgin being touched for the first time. It felt so good for her she clenched his ears and twisted them back, causing him a bit of pleasure and pain.

Moments later she was underneath him biting his shoulder as her body quivered during her orgasm.

After their love making, D'neen snuggled up next to Charles. She had something on her mind, and he could sense it.

"What's on your mind baby?" Charles asked.

"Nothing," D'neen said unconvincingly.

"What is it?"

"Do you think Ashley likes you?"

Charles started to laugh but he knew that this was the time to secure his wife's feelings.

"Baby, it doesn't matter if a thousand women were interested in me, I'm where I want to be."

D'neen smiled. His words were comforting so she fell asleep feeling that her marriage was safe and no one, including Ashley, could come between them.

***

Next door, Ashley got out of bed naked and walked to the bathroom. The handsome guy from the wedding laid in bed admiring her body. He couldn't wait to fuck her again. She was an animal, he thought as he laid naked underneath the covers. Ashley returned wearing a bathrobe.

"Come back to bed," The man said opening the covers revealing himself. Ashley looked at him and smiled. The sex was good, she reflected, and she was up for another round. But she had rules and was determined to stick to them.

"Karl you were good, but it's time for you to go," Ashley said with a smile.

Karl looked at his watch. “It’s 3:00 a.m.”

“And your car is still working, isn’t it?” Ashley said as she sat in a chair.

Karl sat upright in the bed a moment then got up and started dressing.

“It’s not you, I just like to wake up in my bed alone.”

“I understand.”

Karl kissed Ashley on her cheek then left. Ashley laid in bed thinking Karl might be good to keep around a little while.

***

Across town, Tasha laid in bed alone. She couldn’t sleep and was miserable. She had hoped to reconcile with Bruce after the wedding, but seeing Ashley, and how beautiful she was, Tasha had forgotten her plan of reconciliation. Now she didn’t know what she was going to do about Bruce. What made matters worse, her daughter had cried everyday for her daddy since he had been kicked out of the house.

As Tasha laid there, she started doing what she did best, tearing herself down. Before she fell asleep, she was considering plastic surgery.

CHAPTER 9

When Ashley arrived at her studio for work, the intern who usually had her coffee waiting wasn't there and Ashley was pissed. She made a mental note to give the girl a tongue lashing when she saw her.

As Ashley opened the door to enter the studio, she overheard her name mentioned by one of two female interns walking by. Ashley turned around and addressed the woman she believed mentioned her name.

"Did I hear my name come out your mouth?" Ashley said snobbishly.

The two women stopped, caught off guard. The intern who had uttered Ashley's name hesitated a moment then said, "Yeah, I was telling Louise about your show with D'neen."

"What about it?"

"Nothing really, I was just saying D'neen sounded good on the air."

From the look on Ashley' face, the intern knew that Ashley didn't like the fact that at least one person at the station thought D'neen's performance on the show was worthy of conversation.

Ashley was prepared to berate the intern when a man with wide eyes and dressed in a worn tuxedo appeared from out of nowhere and accosted her.

"I set the wedding date for the 10th, I contacted your parents and mine, everyone's going to be there," the man said stammering.

The two interns exchanged nervous looks, but Ashley looked unaffected.

"I got my tux cleaned and I need your size so I can pick up your dress baby," the man said calmly as he gazed into Ashley's eyes.

Ashley turned towards one of the women, "Louise, why don't you get a tape measure so I can take my size," Ashley said sounding sincere.

"Yeah, we have to get your size," the man chimed in nodding his head looking at Louise.

Louise got the cue and walked briskly down the hall. Ashley and the other intern kept their cool while the man yammered away about his and Ashley's wedding and how he was looking forward to the honeymoon. His eyes where filled with excitement when he said he was also looking forward to taking Ashley's virginity.

The intern laughed inside. For a moment she actually felt sorry for the poor guy who thought Ashley was still a virgin. The only thing left tight on Ashley was the space between her teeth, the intern wanted to tell the man.

Moments later, Ashley saw two burly security personnel creeping up behind the man. She touched the man's cheek to distract him. Just as the man was about to complement Ashley on how soft her hand felt, the security personnel seized him and wrestled him to the floor. When they stood him up, Ashley stepped forward and kneed the man hard in the balls.

The man grunted in pain and tilted forward. He would have kneeled over if it wasn't for the support of the two security guys holding him up.

"That's wasn't necessary!" One security guard yelled.

"He probably liked it," Ashley shot back.

Ashley felt exhilarated as any woman would feel who kneed a guy in the balls and got away with it. Security muscled the guy away kicking, screaming, and professing his love for Ashley. The two interns walked away just before D'neen rushed over to Ashley.

"Who was that?" D'neen asked.

"How the hell did he get out of jail," Ashley snapped, not addressing anyone specifically.

"You knew that guy?" D'neen asked more demanding of an answer this time.

"He's one of my stalkers," Ashley said nonchalantly, but almost proudly. "I tried to be nice by getting the law involved, but now think I'm going to have to call my boys to get his mind right."

A station boss walked over and placed his hand on Ashley's shoulders, "You okay?"

"Yeah, thanks."

The boss touched Ashley's chin softly then walked away, but not before nodding his head at D'neen. This was the first time Ashley witnessed one of the bosses acknowledging an intern which caused Ashley to raise an eyebrow.

"Be careful Ashley," D'neen said.

Ashley looked at D'neen remembering the conversation she had with the interns before the stalker interrupted. Ashley was about to question D'neen about the station gossip she just got wind of, but decided to wait because she was running late to go on the air.

"We all have to be careful around here," Ashley said as she entered her studio. D'neen was left dumbfounded wondering what Ashley was hinting at.

Ashley sat down, pulled her microphone close, then clicked it on.

"Hey, your girl Ashley's here and I got a lot of rap for you. First, y'all almost lost your girl for the day, my stalker showed up at the station. I might have to start covering up this beautiful ass of mine, because now I got the crazies chasing it. Yeah, my stalker wanted to get married and deflower your girl. Somebody tell me what they think about that."

Ashley plugged a female caller in.

"If he thought you were a virgin he had to be crazy."

"Yeah you're right, because the only thing tight on me are my pockets because your man keeps stuffing them with money, stop hating and get your hair done," Ashley said then clicked on another female caller.

"Hey Ash," the caller said in a young and timid voice.

"Hey sweetheart. You sound pretty young, how old are you?"

"Nineteen."

"Are you sure?"

The caller chuckled softly, "Yes, I get that a lot."

"What's on your mind girlfriend, you don't sound too happy."

"It's my boyfriend. Our relationship was good then all of a sudden he doesn't seem to like being around me as much as before."

"Did you have sex with him?"

"He was my first, now he's different."

"This is a no brainier. He tells you he's just hanging with his boys, right?"

"How did you know?"

"He's seeing someone else."

Ashley waited for the caller to respond but she didn't. Ashley figured the girl was probably crying.

"Listen sweetheart, you sound like a beautiful young lady, the guy is no good for you. I'll send you ten dollars to dump him because that's what's he's worth. Let him go, it's going to hurt at first but in the long run you'll feel better."

"Thanks Ash," The caller said then hung up.

Ashley went to a commercial then came back on air with a new caller.

"I heard what you told your last caller, I didn't think

you had a heart."

"First time for everything baby."

"For a second I thought you were D'neen --"

Ashley was hot. She clicked the caller off. She made her second mental note of the day and that was to keep an eye on D'neen.

"Friday your girl went to a wedding. There was a chick there, my new friend accidentally spilled a drink on her and she came after your girl like I did it. Imagine me being so childish. Especially in my white Prada gown. I'm not going to tell y'all how much the dress cost because it's already enough hating on me as it is," Ashley said then clicked on the next male caller.

"What were you doing wearing white, it's not like you're pure or anything," The male caller said laughing.

Ashley clicked him off then clicked on a female caller.

"One of these days somebody is going to kick your ass."

"Listen honey, I been through it all: the fights, sugar in the gas tank, lipstick on the windshield, and you know how I responded, I get their men to pay for the damages and put something in my pocket. In fact, I make them pay double. So all you witches out there who are listening, especially those who attend weddings and try to ruin my white Prada gown, cool out, it isn't that serious."

***

Katrina turned off Ashley's show by smashing her radio to the floor. How dare the bitch discuss me on air, Katrina thought angrily.

In the past Katrina had slashed Ashley's car tires and broken a couple of windows, but that was considered an acceptable response to a whore that fucked your husband, Katina concluded.

But exposing the wedding incident and her pain on a

radio show went beyond the call of duty and Ashley Gray must answer for that infraction, Katrina insisted.

Katrina exited her house intending on breaking another one of Ashley's windows but there were children playing in the street, so she went back inside the house.

Katrina went into her bedroom and placed her hands on her hips. Her head was thumping from a headache, the sign that her blood pressure had risen. She knew she needed to calm down, she had to get her fix. She opened the closet and looked at the many dozens of Lewis' designer shirts swinging from the hangers.

After a moment of deciding, she chose an expensive navy blue button down. She grabbed a pair of large scissors from her sewing bag, sat on the edge of the bed and slowly began to cut Lewis' shirt into tiny square pieces.

This was Katrina's therapy, her fix, whenever she reached her boiling point and had to blow off steam. She figured it would be better to cut up a shirt than to carve up Lewis or someone else. But some days she struggled with that decision.

As for Lewis' wardrobe, he wasn't in the habit of wearing the same shirt twice or at least in a six month period, so he didn't notice the decline in the number of shirts he had, and if he had noticed, he never mentioned it to Katrina.

***

Back at the station, the buzz about D'neen's performance on Ashley's show had heightened. Ashley reveled in being the center of attention but now D'neen was unintentionally stealing some of the spotlight.

There were call-ins to hear more of D'neen and Ashley didn't like it. There were even rumors that D'neen was soon to be offered her own show, one that would be wholesome, in contrast to Ashley's, to bring some competitive balance to the airways.

The idea of bringing another female radio personality onto Ashley's domain was an affront to her, provoking Ashley's territorial instinct, which meant bad news for D'neen.

As D'neen conversed with a group of interns, Ashley spied her from across the room. It killed Ashley to witness the accolades bestowed upon D'neen for holding her ground against her.

Ashley never displayed open resentment towards another woman or any cattiness, but she felt like scratching and she had a kitten in her sight.

Ashley pondered what punishment would be fitting for this apple pie bitch. She could invite D'neen out for drinks with a male friend, just the three of them. Before the night was over, a roofie would be put in D'neen's drink and later Ashley would film her friend fucking D'neen and the apple pie bitch would be at Ashley's mercy.

But Ashley knew a plan like that had too many flaws. D'neen could go to the police and have her blood tested and file rape charges. And Ashley was living too high to sign herself up for a prison sentence, so she scrapped that plan.

Ashley's next thought was to seduce Charles and have D'neen walk in on them, just like she had done with Katrina and Lewis. But Ashley didn't like that plan as well, because D'neen was so gullible, she would probably forgive Charles on the spot.

While Ashley pondered D'neen's demise, she didn't notice D'neen walking toward her until she was standing in front of her.

"Hey Ashley, what's up?" D'neen said with a smile.

"Just putting a plan together in my head," Ashley said returning the smile.

"I love it when a plan comes together."

"You do uh?" Ashley said as she chuckled softly.

"Ashley, I was wondering, and I hope I'm not out of line, but I think you and I should do another show. I heard the ratings were off the chains."

Ashley was steaming as she thought, I can't believe this audacious bitch. First, the bitch thinks she's going to get ahead off my back, then the bitch uses a played out phrase such as, off the chain.

At that moment Ashley made up her mind that she was going to fuck Charles, "yeah, we can do another show," Ashley said calmly.

"Thanks."

As D'neen walked away Ashley told herself that she was going to have to cut off one of the men in her life to devote her energy in ruining D'neen's life.

CHAPTER 10

Ashley pulled her car into her driveway. As she exited the car, she saw Charles approaching his house.

"Hey Charles," Ashley shouted over to him.

Charles turned around and gave her a lukewarm wave. She was about to blow a kiss to him, but dismissed the notion as being to presumptuous for her mission. The moment it took for her to cogitate a scheme to get Charles in her house was a moment too long. Charles entered his house and closed the door behind him.

"Shit," Ashley said, then sighed.

She knew she missed an opportunity because Charles and D'neen were rarely apart.

Ashley went into her house. Ten minutes later she was basking in a bubble bath. She laid her head back against the tub, closed her eyes, and pictured in her mind how she was going to straddle Charles, and the look of hurt D'neen would have when she discovered the two of them. The thought gave her a twitch between her legs.

Acting on the sudden sexual urge, Ashley finished her bath and called Karl. She told him to come over her house immediately and the front door will be open.

***

Tasha sat across the table from Katrina in a small diner. Both women appeared to be suffering from jealous woman syndrome, displaying noticeable symptoms. Their eyes were puffy red from too much crying; red noses from too much blowing, they toyed with their food, and the most noticeable sign, whenever a beautiful woman walked by their table they glared at the woman as if she were sleeping with their husbands.

"After what happened at the wedding, Bruce had the nerve to call me asking if he could sleep on the couch until he got his own place."

"Are you going to let him?"

"I don't know…my daughter keeps asking about him."

From past experience, Katrina knew that Bruce would be back in the house.

"After you left the wedding me and Ashley got into it, she spilled a drink on me. I'm thinking about stabbing her."

Tasha stared at Katrina searching her face for a hint that suggested that Katrina was joking, but Tasha saw nothing but earnestness in Katrina's eyes, which scared her little.

"Tasha, I know what you're thinking. I do want to stab her, but in the meantime, I've been taking out my frustrations by cutting up Lewis' shirts," Katrina said with a smile.

"Do you ever think he's still sleeping with her?"

"No, he wouldn't do that to me again."

***

On the other side of the city in a five-star hotel room, Lewis laid on the bed stripped down to his boxers, awaiting the arrival of Ashley who was expected in five minutes.

Lewis actually felt guilt for what he was about to do, but he blamed Katrina for his actions. If she was more affectionate he would have rejected Ashley's advances.

Lewis' mind was in ambivalence, he couldn't wait to be inside Ashley, but he also wanted to break off the relationship because it was too dangerous to continue.

As he stared at the 1930's Circa 18 KYG & platinum bracelet with 52 diamonds he had brought for Ashley, he was beginning to hope she wouldn't show. But that prospect vanished when Ashley entered wearing 3 inch heels and a red silk dress.

Damn she looks good! Lewis thought with his dick as it rose underneath the covers. Ashley saw his impression on the covers and smiled. She gave him a lascivious leer slowly turning her back to him, allowing her dress to drop to the floor. Lewis stared at Ashley's ass and was glad he chased it.

If Lewis was serious about dumping Ashley, he didn't show it as she climbed in bed next to him.

"Here baby."

Lewis put the bracelet on Ashley's wrist then made passionate love to her like he never had before. With each slow stroke, he told himself that he could never let her go.

Twenty minutes later Lewis was shocked when Ashley climbed out of bed and told him that she didn't want to see him again.

"Why."

"I'm afraid of your wife," Ashley said as she slipped on her dress,

Lewis didn't doubt that Ashley was afraid of Katrina because he himself was afraid of her, but the question he asked himself, was fear the only reason for Ashley to dump him?

"In three weeks I have business in Miami, I want you to come with me."

"I can't baby, I don't trust Katrina. She's crazy."

Ashley wanted to tell Lewis that past experience taught her not to fuck with men who live on the same block because things could get messy, because men can be as jealous as women. Pin two jealous men against one another and that could be murderous, a mentor once told Ashley.

"Please baby lets talk about it," Lewis said almost

begging.

"No, its over," Ashley said sharply as she walked towards the door.

"Give me back my bracelet," Lewis yelled.

Ashley opened the door, stopped, then turned around facing Lewis.

"Shut the fuck up," Ashley said, then slammed the door behind her as she left.

CHAPTER 11

Ashley put in motion her plan to seduce Charles. She began by asking D'neen personal questions about him. She was careful not to arouse D'neen's suspicion.

On a Saturday afternoon, Ashley felt her moment to seduce Charles had arrived. D'neen had mentioned that she was going shopping and asked Ashley to join her, but the seductress denied the invitation. Ashley made up an excuse to stay home.

After D'neen had driven away, Ashley waited. She stood in her living room peering out her window when the object of her scheme, Charles, finally pulled his car to the curb in front of his house. Just as Charles emerged from his car he saw Ashley walking towards him.

"What's up Ashley?"

"I've been moving this stuff in the house and I hurt my back. I was looking for D'neen to help but she isn't home and I need to get this done right away."

Charles hesitated a moment, then volunteered his services. As he followed Ashley into her house, Katrina was pulling her car into her driveway. Katrina saw the door close behind them and was stunned by their daylight brazenness.

Katrina wondered if Lewis had lied to her when he swore on his mother that he had never stepped foot in Ashley's house. Katrina slammed the car door and decided to wait outside for the cheaters to emerge. That way, when she told D'neen what she had seen, Charles couldn't deny it.

Inside Ashley's house, Charles stood in the living room checking out the place, he admired Ashley's taste. When Ashley told him that the chest she needed to move was in her bedroom, Charles paused with indecision.

Charles wasn't naïve. It crossed his mind that Ashley had an agenda when she approached him outside, but he gave her the benefit of the doubt because he knew how close she and D'neen had become.

But now he was following her upstairs. He tried, but failed to avert his eyes from watching her ass sway as she mounted the stairs. Charles thought about Ashley's radio show topic, why do men chase women? Look at this ass. Staring at Ashley's ass he could see why, but then he thought of D'neen's pretty face and knew he wasn't going to do anything inappropriate.

When Charles entered Ashley's bedroom and looked at her bed with the red satin sheets, he felt two things: guilt, because he knew he was standing on forbidden grounds, and the swelling inside his pants. He thought about kittens playing, trying to reverse the affect of being turned on.

Ashley pointed to the bed. Charles swallowed hard, thinking that she was about to order him to undress, crawl in bed, and bang her brains out.

"The chest is on the other side of the bed," Ashley said, breaking Charles' erotic thoughts.

When he walked to the other side of the bed and saw the chest, he couldn't believe it was there. He had to get his mind out of the gutter he thought.

Charles reached down to lift the chest. Before he could get to it, Ashley was behind him with one hand rubbing his back and the other cupping his penis.

Outside, Katrina still had Ashley's house under surveillance when she saw D'neen's car drive up and park behind Charles' car. Katrina marched over to D'neen's car. Before D'neen could get out, Katrina was opening the car door like a valet. D'neen looked alarmed as she slowly got out the car.

"Charles is in Ashley's house," Katrina said breathing heavily.

D'neen fought a panic. She didn't want to come off as insecure by jumping to conclusions, then later finding out that the guy who Katrina believed to be Charles was in fact someone else. And if by some reason it was Charles, he was in Ashley's house because there had been an emergency.

When D'neen looked over at Ashley's house and the place wasn't ablaze, D'neen felt sick, "If Charles is in Ashley's house it must be an emergency."

Katrina gave D'neen a look that suggested that D'neen didn't even believe her own words.

"Come on, we're going over there!"

"No, I trust Charles."

"Do you trust Ashley?"

Katrina grabbed hold of D'neen's arm to drag her along if needed, but force wasn't necessary as they marched over to Ashley's house.

Back in Ashley's bedroom, Charles turned around facing Ashley removing her hands from his back and penis. He looked shocked as he opened his mouth to speak, but Ashley halted his words by thrusting her tongue in his mouth. Instincts caused him to kiss her back, but five seconds later he came to his senses and backed away. Ashley was staring at him with lust in her eyes.

"I didn't come here for this," Charles said raising his hands to keep Ashley at bay.

"He did," Ashley said pointing at Charles' crotch area.

Again he thought about the kittens playing, trying to reverse his hard-on. Just as Ashley stepped forward and placed her hands on Charles waist, her doorbell rang, saving him from a difficult decision.

"Damn, stay here," Ashley snapped.

Ashley shot out the room and down the stairs. She

opened the front door and was shocked to see Katrina and D'neen standing there. For a moment, no one said a word. Then Katrina gave D'neen a stern look encouraging her to speak.

"Is my husband here?" D'neen asked trying to sound unconcerned.

Ashley looked back over her shoulder then back to D'neen and smiled. D'neen felt her heart kick at her chest.

"I think you should come in," Ashley said as she opened the door wide for D'neen to enter.

D'neen took a step forward and was stopped by Katrina who placed her arm in front of her.

"She'll wait out here, just tell Charles his wife would like to see him," Katrina said glaring into Ashley's eyes.

Ashley rolled her eyes at Katrina. D'neen looked past Ashley and saw Charles descending the stairs and walking towards the door. D'neen and Charles' eyes met. She saw the guilt on his face, and he saw pain wash over her face.

"Excuse me," Charles said as he made his way past Ashley in the doorway. Before he was out of arms reach, Ashley reached out and touched his back gently.

"Thanks Charlie," Ashley said softly.

D'neen was crushed as she turned and walked briskly to her house. Charles turned towards Ashley. He was so angry he couldn't speak, he just shook his head at her then chased after D'neen.

"You are a real whore," Katrina sniped.

Ashley returned the remark by slamming the door in Katrina's face. Ashley sat down on her sofa and laughed. She felt good, she had crushed D'neen and didn't have to sleep with Charles, although she wanted to.

D'neen entered her bathroom and slammed the door behind her. She stood in front of the sink and splashed cold water on her face, mixing the water with her tears.

D'neen stared in the mirror wondering what had she done wrong to make Charles seek the pleasures of another woman, a friend at that. Was it the petty argument they had three days ago over him leaving the toilet seat up? Was it the argument over what they would have for dinner? Was she not pretty enough? D'neen strained her brain trying to pinpoint her shortcomings.

Charles knocked softly on the door then pushed it open and entered. He looked just as hurt as D'neen. As he approached her and placed a consoling hand on her shoulder. She shrugged his hand away then stared at him through the mirror.

"Nothing happened," Charles said looking at D'neen's face through the reflection in the mirror.

"Sure, tell me anything."

"Don't you trust me?"

D'neen didn't answer, she was on the fence with that one. She wanted to trust and believe him, but what was he doing in Ashley's house in the first place she wondered.

"Why were you in her house?" D'neen said turning and looking him in the eye.

"She needed help moving a chest."

D'neen didn't respond, she was weighing his reason in her mind. It made sense, but D'neen was looking for a better excuse. "Of all the men Ashley knows, she asks you, that didn't arouse your suspicion?"

Charles pulled D'neen close and held her tightly in his arms without answering the question. D'neen felt good in his arms, but jealousy whispered into her ear and she couldn't shake the question that was now in her head.

"Where was the chest, in the basement?"

Charles hesitated, "In her bedroom," he said meekly.

"You ain't shit," D'neen shouted as she shoved Charles away from her, then walked out the bathroom.

***

Across the street, Katrina had stormed in the house upset from having Ashley's door slammed in her face. Lewis was in the kitchen stirring a pot on the stove when Katrina stood in the doorway glaring at him. Lewis cut a quick look at her then back to his pot. He wondered if Katrina found out about the affair with Ashley, but he figured she hadn't because if she had, he would be trying to pry a knife out of her hands.

"Are you hungry?" Lewis asked pretending not to notice her anger.

Katrina didn't respond. She grabbed the phone then sat at the table and called Tasha.

"Hey girl, guess whose she's fucking now?"

Katrina spoke intentionally loud enough for Lewis to hear, and he was listening.

"Charles. Can you believe it?"

Lewis was stunned, he dropped his fork.

"I'll stop by later. Yeah, that bitch needs to be corrected. I'll see you later, I want to check on D'neen."

Katrina hung up the phone and looked at Lewis, who tried to look unconcerned by the shocking news he just learned.

"I know you heard me on the phone. I can't believe you stuck your dick in that garbage can."

Lewis sighed then walked out the kitchen, leaving Katrina to believe that he was walking away from a potential argument but in fact he was pissed and jealous that Ashley was sleeping with Charles.

Thirty minutes later Katrina exited her house and saw D'neen sitting in her parked car sobbing. Katrina walked over and asked D'neen to ride with her over to Tasha's house.

CHAPTER 12

D'neen looked like a car wreck when she walked through Tasha's front door. Tasha hugged her tightly and whispered in her ear, "It's going to be okay sweetheart."

D'neen nodded her head and took a seat across from Katrina who was sitting on the sofa.

"Does anybody want something to drink?" Tasha asked.

Both Katrina and D'neen shook their heads, so Tasha sat next to Katrina.

"So Ashley struck again?" Tasha asked.

D'neen lowered her head.

"We have to correct that bitch. First she fucked my husband, then Tasha's, now she's sleeping with Charles," Katrina said shaking her head pitifully.

"Charles did not sleep with Ashley," D'neen said defensively.

Katrina and Tasha exchanged a look. D'neen caught the exchange and sighed impatiently.

"Let's get down to business," Katrina said authoritatively.

D'neen looked surprised as she asked, "What business are you talking about?"

"You didn't tell her?" Tasha directed to Katrina.

Katrina opened her mouth to speak but didn't have a response.

"We are meeting to discuss what we're going to do

about Ashley," Tasha said.

D'neen stood up, "I'm leaving, I don't want to talk about Ashley or any kind of plot or plan to get her back, and my husband did not sleep with her."

Katrina walked over to D'neen and reached out and took D'neen's hands in her own.

"Please don't go. Every one of us has cried over something Ashley Gray has done to us. If you believe your husband didn't sleep with her, then he didn't. But she was wrong to invite him into her house, it's time she paid. Please hear us out?"

D'neen looked to Tasha and back to Katrina, pondered a moment, then sat down to Katrina and Tasha's delight.

"I think we should open this meeting by each of us saying fuck Ashley," Katrina said with a grin.

D'neen and Tasha smiled. Five seconds later the three women said, "Fuck Ashley," in unison.

"The floor is open for suggestions," Katrina said.

"I say we get fifty guys to gang bang the bitch, videotape it, and put it on the internet," D'neen offered.

Katrina and Tasha exchanged surprising looks.

"Good suggestion, but I'm not going to jail for that bitch," Tasha said.

"Shit, she'd probably like it –We can put on masks and beat the shit out of her," Katrina proposed.

"I agree," Tasha said jumping in.

"No, I can't do that," D'neen said.

"What about poisoning her?" Katrina said with a gleam in her eyes.

"No, nothing like that," D'neen said.

"She doesn't have to die," Katrina offered, "what about paying a cute guy with AIDS--"

"Katrina!" Tasha said sharply.

"Okay, Okay, I'll tone it down."

For over an hour the women laughed and debated a

fitting punishment for Ashley that they could all agree on. Failing to agree, they decided to adjourn their meeting for the night. Before they departed they vowed that before the week was out they would inflict some sort of punishment on Ashley.

CHAPTER 13

Ashley awoke feeling upbeat. She showered, dressed, then headed for work. While Ashley was caught up in her vainglorious world, she had no idea that with each day that passed, three scornful women plotted how to bring the diva to her knees.

As she pulled her car into the radio station's parking lot, her cell phone rang. She killed the ignition and grabbed her phone. Before she answered she looked at the phone number, it was one she didn't recognize. Usually she wouldn't answer an unknown number, but today she did.

"Hey," Ashley said jollily into the phone.

When the person on the other end spoke, Ashley grimaced. It was a voice from her past, one she hadn't heard in ten years. Her first thought was, how did this bitch get my number? Her next thought was, what does my mother want?

"What do you want?" Ashley asked with an unfriendly tone. There was silence, Ashley's mother hesitated then said, "I wanted to say hello, I miss you…and I'm very sick."

Ashley responded by hanging up. There were serious issues between Ashley and her mother, and now that she was famous she wasn't going to let her mother in her life regardless of how sick she was. You should've been there when I needed you bitch, Ashley thought as she choked back tears.

Ashley gathered herself and entered the station. She

had twenty minutes before she was due to go on air so she killed the time by entertaining the conversation of a guy trying to get in her pants.

Although the guy didn't have a chance Ashley listened to his tired rap to get her mind off of the phone call from her mother.

Two minutes into the conversation Ashley's cell phone rang, she looked at the number and sighed.

"I'll talk to you later," Ashley said to the guy as she walked away. She answered the phone, it was Lewis.

Ashley listened as he yelled through the phone at her for dumping him for Charles. He threatened to kick both Ashley and Charles' ass. Ashley laughed then hung up.

The Lewis phone call triggered thoughts of Charles, he was the only man ever to rebuff her advances. He's a good guy Ashley thought.

For the first time in Ashley's adult life she felt remorse for trying to seduce a man to hurt his woman.

Ashley hadn't spoken with D'neen since the day of the attempted seduction and today she wanted to apologize, so she went looking for D'neen.

Since D'neen discovered Charles in Ashley's house she had successfully avoided Ashley in the neighborhood and at work, but her success came to an end in the ladies room at the radio station.

D'neen was in a stall using the toilet. After she finished her business, she opened the stall door to exit and saw Ashley blocking the door with her arms folded across her chest.

"You have been avoiding me. I just want to tell you that nothing happened between Charles and me."

"Excuse me," D'neen said.

Ashley stepped to the side as D'neen headed to the sink and washed her hands. Ashley walked over and stood behind D'neen.

"I know I have a reputation, but I don't cross my

friends."

"Was Katrina a friend?"

"That was five years ago."

D'neen turned around and glared into Ashley's eyes and said, "You were a whore then and you're still one today."

As D'neen smirked, Ashley slapped her hard across the face and pushed D'neen back against the sink. D'neen grunted in pain then charged Ashley who stepped to the side. D'neen went falling into the stall with her hand landing into the toilet bowl.

D'neen was incensed. With rage in her eyes she stood ready for battle. Ashley too was poised for a fight as she clenched her fist and stepped forward towards D'neen. Two women entered the bathroom.

Ashley unclenched her fist and smiled at D'neen, awaiting her next move. D'neen thought about finishing the fight, but decided now wasn't time so she stormed out the bathroom, out the building, and into her car.

Ashley marched out and went straight to her studio, five minutes later she was on the air.

"Hey, your girl Ash has a lot to talk about today. It's amazing how many women are insecure these days. If I want a guy, I get the guy, okay. I'm just letting you squares out there know what time it is," Ashley said cockily as she clicked on a female caller.

"Ashley I am definitely feeling you."

"Thank you girlfriend. If a woman holds a man too tightly she can squeeze him right out of her hand and into mine."

"Ashley, who is your latest victim?"

"I won't call him a victim, but I had this guy over the house the other night. He lives on my block, let's call him Chuck. And for the record, big bad Ashley didn't twist his arm to get him over, okay?"

"Is he married?"

"He wasn't behaving like a married man that day?"

"I know the type girlfriend."

"Anyway, we were making out, kissing, touching, getting into it, when the door bell rang. I answered the door and who's standing there, his wife and her sidekick."

"Ouch."

"Don't worry about me, I know how to handle myself. Well let me end by saying Chuck left with his wife, but he and I are still good friends, wink, wink."

***

D'neen, who was driving and listening to Ashley's show, got into a fender bender. After D'neen and the other driver exchanged insurance information, she hopped back in her car and sped home.

D'neen pulled her car to a screeching halt in her driveway knocking over two trash cans. She hopped out the car and darted into the house.

"Charles, Charles!"

There was no answer. She rushed upstairs into the bedroom, it was empty. She sat on the edge of the bed and cried.

Ten minutes later Charles entered, D'neen jumped in his face, "You fucked her!"

Charles was caught off guard, "What are you talking about?"

"Ashley, you fucking liar," D'neen said with spit foaming on the side of her mouth.

"I thought we were past this, and no I didn't fuck her."

"But she said on the radio--"

Charles pulled D'neen close to him, "Are you going to believe that whore over me? We can't let that liar come between us. She's fucking with your head."

D'neen thought about it, and remembered how

Ashley taunted people on her show. D'neen began to feel sorry for accusing Charles. And he could see it in her face so he kissed her.

"She can't come between us D'neen."

"I know, but when she said y'all was kissing I lost it."

D'neen saw what appeared to be a twitch in Charles' face when she mentioned that he and Ashley were kissing. She almost dismissed it, but something pushed her to ask, "Did you kiss her?"

Charles hesitated. He never lied to D'neen and at the moment he debated whether to tell her the truth.

"Did you kiss her?"

"She uh, kissed me," Charles said barely above a whisper.

A tear fell from D'neen's eye. He pulled her close and wrapped his arms around her tightly, "I love you baby, I love only you."

D'neen didn't respond. Her stomach was weak and it felt like a softball was in her throat. She pictured Charles pounding Ashley from behind. The thought made her sick, she pushed him away from her then walked to the dresser and started snatching his clothes from the drawers, tossing them on the bed.

"What are you doing?" Charles asked.

"One of us is not sleeping here tonight."

***

Later that night Ashley laid in her bed next to Karl. After their sex, she felt so satisfied, she decided to break her rule, and asked him to stay the night. He obliged by making love to her until both of them fell asleep from exhaustion.

Next door D'neen laid in bed staring at the ceiling. Charles had left the house, but didn't take any clothing because he insisted that he was coming back tomorrow once

D'neen had cooled down.

D'neen had tried to sleep but it had eluded her. This was the first night she would spend alone since she had been married, and she wasn't used to sleeping alone.

Restless, she sat up, turned on the television, then turned it off a minute later. She then went to the kitchen.

Once in the kitchen she sat at the table and ate from a pint of ice cream. She had only been married a couple months and now she was seeking comfort in food to help cope with the stress of a failing marriage.

D'neen then had a thought. She sat her spoon down, and smiled. She went down into the basement and grabbed a gallon of black paint and a paintbrush.

Three minutes later with a baseball cap pulled down obstructing her face, D'neen stood in front of Ashley's garage. D'neen looked both ways up and then down the street, it was deserted. She dipped her brush in the paint. What came next were the words: A WHORE LIVES HERE, on Ashley's garage.

D'neen then darted in her house. She closed her door behind her and leaned against it, panting as if she was running away from committing murder.

D'neen peeked out the window, the street was still empty. She checked nearby houses, there were no lights on from a nosey neighbor. She then went upstairs, hopped in the bed, and surprisingly, ten minutes later she was sound asleep.

CHAPTER 14

It was 7:00 a.m., sunny, and seasonally warm when Ashley and Karl exited her house from a night of wild sex and little sleep. Karl reached out and took Ashley's hand in his own.

The move caught Ashley by surprise because she wasn't the hand holding type. She thought about withdrawing her hand but decided against it since they were only walking to the car.

When they approached the garage they were stunned as they stared at D'neen's paint job. Ashley squeezed Karl's hand in anger. She looked around as if she expected to see the culprit running down the street with a gallon of paint in one hand and the dripping paint brush in the other.

"How could someone do something so childish?" Karl said speaking out loud but not directly to Ashley.

Ashley placed her hands on her hips and glared at Katrina's house for a moment then turned her attention next door to D'neen's house. Ashley figured the guilty party resided on her block.

Ashley's first thought was to knock on D'neen's door, and when she answered, pull her out into the middle of the street and whip her ass. After the bathroom incident, Ashley was confident that she could handle D'neen with no problem.

On the other hand, if Katrina was responsible for the painting, things would have to be handled differently. Ashley thought back five years earlier when she had mouthed off to Katrina. Before Ashley had time to react, Katrina's hands were wrapped around Ashley's neck like a python snake. If Lewis hadn't pulled Katrina away from Ashley only God knows what would've happened.

"I can paint over it for you, do you have any paint?" Karl asked.

The question brought Ashley back to the present. She wondered how Karl felt about someone accusing her of being a whore. Ashley was surprised by her thought, because for the first time in her life, she cared how she was being perceived by a man.

"I'll call a painter and get the whole garage repainted. But thanks for offering."

Twenty minutes later the painter arrived, he smiled when he saw the garage. When Karl wasn't paying attention, the painter gave Ashley a soliciting look. She sneered at the painter as if he was beneath her.

"I know one of those bitches on this block did this," Ashley snapped at Karl.

"How can you be sure?"

"I know," Ashley said with certainty, knowing what she had done to cause the insult against her in the first place.

"It could've been anyone, you annoy a lot of people with your radio show."

Ashley never spoke with Karl about her show nor had he mentioned that he ever listened to it. Again, she began to wonder how he felt about someone accusing her of being a whore.

Karl gave Ashley a smile and touched her chin softly with his hand. At that moment Ashley felt something growing in her heart for Karl that gave her butterflies in her stomach. She had never felt these feelings for any man before, she knew it was love, and that scared her. So she attempted to fan the flames growing in her heart by redirecting her anger towards Karl, "I'm not a whore, and if you think I am you can leave," Ashley said scowling in Karl's face.

Karl looked startled as he responded, "I haven't accused you of anything, and I'm not the enemy."

Gathering herself quickly, Ashley placed her hand on Karl's shoulder and said, "I'm sorry, but these bitches on this block hate me and I'm angry right now!"

Karl patted Ashley on her butt, "It's okay, I understand."

The pat on the butt caused Ashley's pussy to twitch, something that had never happened before. She told herself, get it together girl.

When the painter finished repainting the garage, Karl paid him. The painter walked to his van, but not before giving Ashley another soliciting look. Ashley rolled her eyes then walked up to the van and whispered to the painter, "You can't afford me."

Ashley walked back over to Karl and said, "Let's go to breakfast."

After Karl and Ashley got into their own cars and drove away, D'neen emerged from her house with a smile. She then walked over to Katrina's house and rang the bell. Katrina opened the door surprised to see D'neen.

"What's up?" Katrina asked.

"Nothing. I just wanted to know if you want to go out for breakfast, we can give Tasha a call to join us."

***

Over at Tasha's house, she and her daughter were heading out the house when Bruce walked up as they were leaving. The daughter ran over to Bruce and jumped into his arms.

"Daddy!"

"Hey baby girl." Bruce then turned his attention towards Tasha, "Baby I want to come home."

Before Tasha could respond, her daughter asked,

"Mommy why can't daddy come home?"

Tasha was flabbergasted. She wanted to tell the little girl, because daddy likes to stick his dick in other women, but she held that remark, then uttered to Bruce, "Let's go inside and talk?"

Bruce kissed his daughter and smiled as he followed Tasha back into the house. Before Bruce could sit his daughter down, she said, "Daddy, mommy had her friends over and they was talking about this lady."

Tasha was shocked. She was about to admonish her daughter when her cell phone rang. She answered the phone, it was Katrina on the other end.

"Hey girl. No I can't, I have Bruce here and I might have to smack this little snitch on her ass. Yeah, she's developed quite a tongue. I'll tell you later, okay bye." Tasha hung up the phone and glared at her daughter.

"You had company?" Bruce asked.

"Don't question me about what I do in my own house. If you want to talk, we can talk?"

***

Twenty minutes later Katrina and D'neen walked into the same restaurant where Ashley and Karl were finishing their breakfast. Katrina and D'neen sat at a table near the door and placed their order. As Karl and Ashley headed towards the door, Ashley stopped in front of Katrina and D'neen's table.

"I know it was you," Ashley said addressing D'neen.

D'neen smiled, "You knew it was me that did or said what?"

"This is easier to remove than paint," Ashley said as she picked up a glass of orange juice from the table and tossed it in D'neen's face.

"Bitch!" D'neen ripped as she stood abruptly.

Karl separated the two women, who were both yelling threats and insults past Karl stuck in the middle of them.

Finally Katrina placed her hand on D'neen's forearm, and whispered in D'neen's ear, "Now is not the time."

D'neen slowly calmed down but she was still breathing heavily. Ashley also calmed down.

"Thank you," Karl said to Katrina.

Karl reached into his pocket and removed three twenty dollar bills and tossed them on table, "Breakfast is on me. Let's go Ashley."

Ashley shot D'neen a look then walked briskly out the restaurant with Karl following.

"Don't worry, we're going to get her," Katrina said smiling.

In the parking lot, Karl opened Ashley's car door for her. She climbed behind the wheel then smiled at him, "I'm okay."

"You take care of yourself and call me later, okay?"

"Okay," Ashley said starting the ignition.

Ashley drove away making her first stop at a clothing store, buying three expensive dresses. Her next destination was a gun store. She wanted to purchase a 9 mm on the spot but was told she had to wait for the background check. She left the store with pepper spray.

As Ashley sat in a traffic jam, she thought about Karl. He had touched a place in her that no other man had touched before. When the traffic finally freed, Ashley drove to Karl's work and gave him a spare key to her house. The move shocked him as well as Ashley herself.

Later that day Ashley looked at her calendar. She thought about her period. It was late, but she wasn't concerned because her cycle had been screwed up for the past ten years, she figured it should be on any day now.

Ashley also thought about her mother and whether she should visit her or not. Ashley convinced herself that if she did go to see her mother it wouldn't be out of concern for her mother's health, but for the sole purpose of spitting in her face.

CHAPTER 15

"Okay, you can sleep on the couch. Now I have to get to work," Tasha told Bruce.

"Thanks baby, we'll take things slow," Bruce said walking Tasha to the door.

"We're not taking anything slow, you are on the couch until you find a place."

Bruce nodded his head knowing that once he was back in the house he was back in Tasha's life. Tasha opened the door to leave. Bruce reached out and placed his hand upon her shoulder, she turned to face him.

"I swear to God, I'll never hurt you again. I'd rather die than bring you that kind of pain again," Bruce said earnestly. He gazed into Tasha's eyes, she held his gaze.

Bruce's words froze Tasha in her place. He had touched her and knew it, so he took the opportunity to kiss her on her cheek. Tasha formed a slight smile, "Don't let the baby eat what she wants, give her real food," Tasha said then left.

As Tasha drove to work she thought maybe this time Bruce was telling the truth and Ashley, nor any other woman, will come between her and Bruce ever again.

***

After Ashley placed her house key in Karl's hand and left, he called his wife and told her he wanted a divorce. He then placed another call to Ashley just to tell her that he loved her.

Later, Karl caught the jewelry store open fifteen minutes before closing time. He wanted to see their engagement rings. He wouldn't be buying today, but he told the clerk that he would be back in a day or two.

Since Ashley dropped the key in Karl's hand his head had been spinning. He had only known Ashley a month, but he knew he wanted to spend the rest of his life with her and believed that she felt the same.

***

Charles walked out of the gift shop at the mall with two white "His" and "Hers" Teddy Bears and ten greeting cards. They all sent the same message, "I'm sorry."

While he sat in the food court eating a slice of pizza a woman approached him. She was beautiful and straight forward when she asked for his number. Charles immediately thought about Ashley and told the woman he was married. She responded by saying, "What does your wife have to do with me?"

"I guess your name is Ashley, uh?" Charles quipped, believing that Ashley was probably behind the woman's advances.

"My name's not Ashley, but your fine ass can call me whatever you want."

The woman wrote her number down on a piece of paper, and as a joke, she listed her name as Ashley. She handed the number to Charles and walked away.

Charles looked at the number, then around the food court expecting to see Ashley, but she was nowhere to be seen. Charles finished his pizza and stood to leave, then pondered a moment as he picked up the woman's number and put it in his pocket. He had every intention on giving the number to Ashley and telling her to leave him the fuck alone.

***

Over at Tasha's, Bruce felt that his troubled marriage had finally turned that corner for the better, thanks to the smile Tasha gave him before she left for work earlier that day.

Bruce sat on the sofa and thought about his life, he knew he had to find a job and get his shit together. He dialed a friend and asked for help. His friend responded by offering Bruce a job. Bruce hung up the phone feeling he was on his way.

He thought about the many times he had hurt Tasha and how she always accepted him back. At that moment he made a promise to God that if he cheated again he would ransom his life for his infidelity.

Bruce called his sister who agreed to watch his daughter. He hurried and got his daughter dressed then drove her to his sister's for the night. On his way home Bruce stopped at a red light and thought about how he was going to cater and make love to Tasha when she came home.

***

Ashley and D'neen left out the radio station at the same time with D'neen walking just ahead of Ashley. Neither woman had said a word to the other that day, but there was tension in the air whenever they passed each other, which was several times.

As D'neen walked towards her car, Ashley watched her with hatred. Ashley remembered the pepper spray she bought earlier and removed it from her pocketbook and followed D'neen who was aware she was being pursued.

When D'neen reached her car she spun around to face Ashley who was raising the pepper spray.

"Ashley," Someone called out.

Ashley looked a few parked cars over and saw a woman waving at her. Ashley lowered the pepper spray, sneered at D'neen, then walked to the person who had called her. D'neen hopped in her car and drove away oblivious to the fact that if the woman hadn't called Ashley, she would be on the ground crying and rubbing her eyes fiercely from the effects of the pepper spray.

After speaking with the woman who had interrupted her intended assault upon D'neen, Ashley hopped in her car and sped away.

When Ashley pulled to a red light, she looked to the car next to her and saw Bruce sitting in his car appearing to be in deep thought.

Ashley smiled and honked her horn, snapping Bruce out of his deep thoughts of Tasha. He looked to his left and saw Ashley in her car smiling at him. He nodded at her then looked straight ahead.

Ashley honked her horn again, this time Bruce didn't look in her direction. The light turned green so he pulled off, he felt proud of himself for pretty much ignoring Ashley. When he reached the next intersection he caught another red light. Again Ashley's car drove up next to his.

"Pull over!"

Bruce heard Ashley's voice shouting into his car. When the light turned green, Bruce reluctantly pulled his car to the curb, Ashley parked behind him. They both exited their cars and met on the sidewalk.

"How have you been?" Ashley asked, staring into Bruce's eyes.

"Alright."

"Are you still angry with me?"

"Naw, it's all good."

There was a moment of silence. Ashley looked across the street at nothing in particular then back to Bruce.

"Where are you headed?"

"Home."

"You and wifey back together?"

"Yeah."

"I'm glad to hear that, I hope things work out."

"Me too."

Twenty minutes later in a hotel room, Bruce was banging Ashley from behind. With each stroke he felt as if he was sticking a knife into Tasha's back. He looked at his reflection in the mirror and saw a devil staring back at him, he felt so guilty he couldn't wait to finish. He thrust faster and harder trying to cum. Ashley thought she was the reason for his intensity.

Bruce grunted as he finally came. He dressed quickly and hurried out the hotel room. As he drove home, he hated himself and his lack of self control, once again he was conquered by his lower desires. He smacked the steering wheel hard with his palm, "Stupid, stupid, stupid," he jarred.

Bruce exited the car and went into his house. He showered then laid on the sofa cursing himself until he fell asleep.

***

Charles entered the bedroom while D'neen was in the shower. He placed the Teddy Bears on the bed and the ten greeting cards around the room. He then laid on the bed and waited for D'neen.

When D'neen entered and saw Charles she was a little angry, but when she saw the Teddy Bears her anger withered away. Charles and D'neen didn't have to say a word, their love making did all the talking.

***

When Ashley arrived home, her house was pitch black. But she didn't need the light to find her stairs. As she headed for the stairs, someone grabbed her from behind wrapping their hand around her neck. Ashley froze in fear. Her fear choked her voice from screaming for help.

Ashley remembered the pepper spray. She reached for it but remembered she left it on the passenger seat. She cursed under her breath.

A soft kiss was placed on her cheek, her body

trembled. Her mind raced back to a time when a man she referred to as a monster took her against her will. Her mind then cogitated an escape and survival. She cursed again under her breath for not having the pepper spray. What if this guy has AIDS, she thought.

Ashley was about to elbow her attacker when Karl said, "Hey baby."

"Motherfucker!" Ashley snapped, then elbowed Karl in his stomach.

"Aaaaah."

Ashley faced Karl in the dark, "Good for you, you scared the shit out of me."

"I'm sorry baby."

"How the hell you get in here?"

"You gave me a key."

Ashley made a mental note to take back the key before Karl left. Ashley turned the light on, but Karl turned it off.

"No lights."

He turned Ashley's back to his chest and kissed her neck. Ashley thought about the sex she had with Bruce an hour earlier and it turned her on. Karl unfastened her belt, and slid his hand into her panties, Ashley moaned.

They sank to the carpet floor. Karl laid on his back and pulled Ashley on top of him with her back to his chest. After they made love, they laid quietly in their places while Karl caressed Ashley's breast. Karl thought about asking Ashley to marry him. Ashley thought about Bruce and felt guilty because she really liked Karl.

"I was thinking we should get married," Karl said.

"You're already married."

"I told her I want a divorce."

"I'm going away for a couple of days the day after tomorrow."

"Where are you going?"

"Did you tell your wife you wanted to marry me?

Karl didn't respond, he was wondering why Ashley avoided his question, "I asked you to marry me and you tell me you're going away with someone."

"First of all you didn't ask me to marry you, secondly I didn't say I was going away with anyone."

"So will you marry me?"

Ashley fell silent. She liked Karl but never thought about marrying him or anyone else for that matter, so she lied when she said, "We'll talk about it when I come back from visiting my mother."

"You told me that your mother was dead," Karl said surprisingly.

"I lied. Why would you want to marry a woman who lies to you?"

Karl didn't have an answer, so he laid quietly thinking, did he really know Ashley well enough for marriage. Ashley wondered if she could commit to Karl or any man.

CHAPTER 16

When Tasha entered her house from a hectic shift at the hospital she found Bruce snoring on the couch. He was stripped down to his boxers. Tasha studied his muscular chest for a moment then headed for the stairs. Before she mounted the stairs something inside her caused her to pause. She walked back over to Bruce and watched him sleep and wondered what he was dreaming about, if he was dreaming at all. Tasha's eyes moved to his crotch area. She began to desire Bruce; she wasn't horny, she was just in love with the man asleep on the couch that had broken her heart repeatedly.

Tasha leaned over and kissed Bruce softly on his mouth. She twirled her tongue in his ear awaking him. Bruce first thought it was Ashley, then he realized where he was at when he saw Tasha.

Tasha discovered his chest with her tongue making her way lower and lower. Bruce moaned softly and played in Tasha's hair with his fingers as she pleasured him.

Again he thought about Ashley and the sex and the guilt of what happened earlier. But Tasha was good, her performance chased the thought of Ashley out of Bruce's head. Tasha herself was turned on, her rhythm increased.

Bruce's breathing was erratic and quickened, his pulse quickened, his hips thrust then gyrated. Bruce and Tasha both felt a climax was near. She cut her eyes up at him, his head was tilted back and his eyes were closed.

"Ashley," Bruce muttered as he released.

Just as Tasha tasted Bruce she heard "Ashley." Those words were a brick wall that Tasha's car sped into, the car was totaled. Tasha was benumbed with rage. It took Bruce a moment to realize what he had done, calling out the enemy's name during sex with his wife was unforgivable.

For a moment he thought she would bite off his penis, but she didn't. She stood slowly wiping her mouth with her shirt sleeve. It took strength in Tasha she didn't know she had to fight back the tears. Without giving him a glance, she walked like a zombie towards the stairs. Bruce hopped off the sofa and rushed over to her.

"Baby, I'm sorry. I'm really sorry."

He wrapped his arms around Tasha's waist stopping her, but she didn't speak and didn't attempt to break free from his grasp.

"I need help. I got a job -- I'm going to see someone, I'm going to talk to a professional," Bruce stammered.

Tasha didn't respond, she walked out of his enfold and up the stairs.

Bruce trudged back to the sofa and sat with his face in his hands. Why didn't he run the light when he saw Ashley at the intersection, he thought.

Tasha walked into the bathroom and stared blankly into the mirror. She grabbed the toothpaste and toothbrush and scrubbed her teeth until her gums bled. Five minutes later her mouth still felt dirty. She washed her face -- still no tears. She then walked down the stairs, past Bruce, and out the door without giving him a second look.

Bruce rushed over to the window, looked out, and watched Tasha as she hopped in her car and drove away.

Bruce moved away from the window. He looked around the living room shaking his head, he knew this time he really fucked up. He took a picture of his daughter from off the mantel and walked upstairs. In the bedroom, Bruce packed some clothes. He started to take everything but he held out a pinch of hope that somehow Tasha would forgive him. As he walked down the block away from the house, he hoped that Tasha wouldn't do anything stupid or hurt herself.

CHAPTER 17

Lewis and Katrina were in bed asleep when they were awakened by the ringing of the telephone. Katrina looked at the clock, it was 2:45 a.m. She sighed, then answered the phone.

Tasha was on the other end sobbing and speaking incoherently. Through the mumbling Katrina was able to gather that Bruce had done something horrible and Tasha wanted to meet her at an overnight diner.

Katrina hung up the phone and dressed quickly.

"Where are you going?" Lewis asked frowning.

"Out," Katrina said sarcastically.

Lewis sat upright, "What the fuck you mean out?" He looked at the clock, then back to Katrina, "It's almost 3 o'clock."

"A friend of mine is in trouble and needs my help."

Katrina was about to tell Lewis about Tasha but he interrupted.

"You don't have any friends."

"I did have one, but you fucked her," Katrina said contumely. Before Lewis could respond, Katrina was out the house and in her car.

***

Tasha sat in an overnight diner looking a wreck as she stared into a cup of coffee that had grown cold. Ten minutes later Katrina entered and the two women embraced.

"Are you okay," Katrina asked looking Tasha over.

"No."

"Where's your daughter?"

"Bruce's sister's."

"Let's sit down," Katrina said.

"In all the years Bruce and I had been together and I went down on him, he never came. Which didn't bother me, because I don't particularly like sucking dick -- I don't feel bad, shit I'm not a super-head chick."

Tasha paused, chuckled, then continued almost laughing, "But tonight I thought I was really doing it, until he called out Ashley's name."

"Oh God, no."

"The motherfucker came in my mouth as he moaned that bitch's name! Can you believe that shit? I brushed my teeth three times tonight, flossed, gargled with mouthwash, but I can still taste him," Tasha said shaking her head.

Katrina was speechless. She thought if Lewis had done that to her she would probably be in prison today.

"Can you imagine how I felt? I thought he was feeling me, but the whole time he had his eyes closed picturing that whore in his mind!"

"He ain't shit! I know you're done for good now."

"This time our relationship is broken and can't be fixed. He's gone for good when I get back home."

"Do you want me to go home with you?"

"No, I can handle Bruce."

"What about Ashley?"

"I don't know, maybe we can get together and discuss it with D'neen."

"Fuck D'neen! We don't need her, she's always bitching."

"Let's keep her on the board. Whatever we do with two will be better with three for what I have in mind, but I want to think it over some more before I reveal it."

"Okay, we can get together around noon tomorrow,"

Katrina said smiling.

Five minutes later the women embraced and hopped in their cars and drove away. Katrina went home, but Tasha wasn't ready to go back home and confront Bruce, so she drove aimlessly around the city thinking.

Tasha felt like a fool for the years she had taken care of Bruce; washed his dirty underwear, and he repaid her by calling out Ashley's name during oral sex. The thought of it made Tasha want to vomit.

Tasha began to blame herself for her predicament. She knew about Bruce's reputation when she married him, but like so many women, she thought she could change him. She laughed and sobbed as she remembered telling her sister that a married man only cheats when his woman isn't taking care of her business at home. How naïve, she thought as she stopped at a red light.

As she waited for the green light, her sadness turned to anger. She wanted Bruce to feel the pain that was assaulting her heart. For the first time in Tasha's marriage she wanted to cheat.

Tasha thought about how guys used to hit on her and how happy she was to decline their advances. She thought about her main pursuer, Vern from work. Every time Bruce had hurt her, Vern always had kind words to offer: "How could anyone hurt someone as wonderful as you --You're gorgeous -- Bruce is such a fool not to realize what he have --If you were my woman I would give you the world."

The words always flattered Tasha, but not enough to convince her to walk away from Bruce into the awaiting arms of Vern.

Tasha looked at the time, it was 3:30 a.m. She knew Vern's shift was over a half hour ago. On an impulse she picked up her cell phone to call him then the light turned green, so she tossed the cell phone into the passenger's seat.

But ten minutes later Tasha sat nervously on the sofa in Vern's apartment. He paced in front of her, his face distorted with anger. Tasha had just told Vern that Bruce had called her Ashley.

"I can't believe he did that! I would never utter an unkind word to you. I'm going to kick Bruce's ass!" Vern ranted.

"No, the relationship is over," Tasha said lowering her head in sadness.

Like a good picker-upper, Vern knew the time for compassion had arrived. He sat silently next to Tasha and gazed in her eyes. She held his gaze for a few seconds then lowered her head. Vern lifted her chin with a soft hand.

"Why would you hide your beautiful face?" Vern said in his most seductive voice.

Tasha didn't respond, she didn't feel beautiful. She wanted to tell him, "No need to lie, you're going to get the pussy, that's why I'm here at 4:00 a.m.," but she held it. Besides, it felt good for someone to call her beautiful.

While Vern made slow love to Tasha, her body responded, but her mind was not in it. Although she had divorced Bruce in mind, body, and soul, she felt like a cheater. Her plan to hurt Bruce only brought her more pain because she wasn't a fan of one night stands.

After the sex Tasha laid next to Vern, he placed his hand on her head and gave her a slight push downward. Tasha knew what he was gesturing at, and it turned her stomach. She moved her head to remove his hand.

Whether Vern got the hint or didn't care, he replaced his hand on her head and gave her head another downward push. The thought of Tasha putting her mouth on another penis made her sick, so sick that she vomited on Vern's chest.

"Bitch what's wrong with you!"

"I'm sorry."

After cursing out Tasha, Vern showered while Tasha got dressed. She knew that coming to his house was a bad decision. She thought about Vern's wooing words, "I would never utter an unkind word to you." Tasha spat on Vern's bed then left his house.

When Tasha returned home she was expecting to see Bruce on his knees begging for forgiveness. But she was pleased to discover that he had left. Tasha made a note to call a locksmith in the morning.

Tasha ran a hot bath. As she basked in the tub, she thought about her life and how in shambles it was. At that moment she made a vow that she would never be with another man again in her life.

CHAPTER 18

Ashley woke to the smell of fried eggs and potatoes and onion floating from the kitchen. She smiled as she rose from the living room floor. She found her panties and blouse and put them on, then walked on her toes barefoot into the kitchen. Karl's back was to Ashley as he stood in front of the stove. Ashley pinched his butt.

"What are you doing?" Ashley asked with her hands on her hips. Karl turned to face her with a plate of food in his hand.

"Good morning baby."

Karl placed the plate on the table, pulled out a chair, and guided Ashley into the chair.

"Thank you," Ashley said smiling.

"I have to run, so I'll see you later," Karl said before giving Ashley a kiss.

"I'll see you later."

Karl handed Ashley a fork then left. Ashley thought, Karl is really making a case for himself. Ashley looked at the food and suddenly felt sickness in her stomach. She rubbed her stomach then rushed to the sink and vomited.

"What the fuck is wrong with me?"

CHAPTER 19

It was a little before noon. Tasha sat on her sofa next to Katrina, who held Tasha's hand in her own.

"You made a mistake, but you can't beat yourself up over it," Katrina said consolingly.

"I can't believe I cheated on Bruce."

"Fuck Bruce! Look at all the times he hurt you."

"Yeah, but cheating is cheating and he's still my husband."

"He's your husband by default."

"You should've seen Vern's face when I threw up on him."

"Good for him, trying to get a blow job knowing you were vulnerable. You should've hurled on his dick."

Breaking the seriousness of the mood. Both Tasha and Katrina laughed. After the laugh, both women went quiet. Tasha started fiddling her fingers.

"Katrina, I'm happy we met and became friends."

"Me too girlfriend."

"Men are dogs, I'm done with them all."

"You just need some time to yourself. When the right person comes along, you'll forget all these problems you had with Bruce."

Tasha smiled, appreciating Katrina's uplifting words. Tasha looked at Katrina admiringly for a moment, and then averted her eyes shyly. Katrina sensed that something was on Tasha's mind and she was having difficulty conveying it.

"What are you thinking?" Katrina asked.

Tasha hesitated, "Katrina -- I uh, you're just wonderful, strong, and beautiful."

"Thank you."

Again Tasha hesitated, "Katrina --"

"What's up?"

Tasha didn't immediately respond. Katrina saw the nervousness in her eyes. When Tasha finally opened her mouth to speak, her words were halted by the doorbell. Tasha actually looked relieved.

"That must be D'neen," Tasha said standing.

"What were you about you say?"

"It wasn't important," Tasha said moving toward and answering the door.

D'neen entered. The two women greeted each other and embraced. D'neen repeated the same greeting with Katrina. The trio then sat down, with D'neen sitting next to Katrina and Tasha sitting across from them. Katrina looked curiously at Tasha who held Katrina's stare for a moment then averted her eyes. The eye exchange between Tasha and Katrina went unnoticed by D'neen.

"What's up?" D'neen said cheerfully.

"We're kidnapping Ashley Gray," Katrina said boldly.

D'neen laughed, then studied the serious faces of Katrina and Tasha. D'neen's cheerfulness recoiled. Katrina gave Tasha the I-told-you-so-look.

"Y'all aren't serious?"

Katrina stood, and with the demeanor of a drill sergeant, she paced in front of D'neen, "We have it all figured out. She will never know it's us. We will wear masks, be clad in black; take Ashley Gray to a cabin upstate then have a little fun as we teach her a lesson."

"Then what, kill her?" D'neen said jumping in.

"Of course not, we're not murderers," Tasha offered with a laugh, trying to downplay the seriousness of the proposal.

"It's all in fun, just over the weekend," Katrina added.

"Charles and I made up last night -- I mean, I don't know about this."

Tasha looked disappointed. Katrina looked disgustedly at D'neen before sitting down. Katrina pondered a moment then stood abruptly, startling D'neen.

"You don't know the meaning of friendship. You're only concerned with yourself. You don't care about Tasha nor me," Katrina said pointing a stern finger in D'neen's face.

"That's not true," D'neen countered.

"Last night while you were enjoying the pleasures of your husband, Bruce called out Ashley's name during sex with Tasha. What do you think about that, Mrs. I made up with my husband last night," Katrina said mockingly.

"I'm sorry," D'neen directed to Tasha.

"Yeah, you're sorry," Katrina said sitting down.

The trio went silent. Each woman was engulfed in her thoughts: Tasha, happy that Katrina didn't reveal to D'neen the entire story of Bruce moaning Ashley's name. Katrina thought of D'neen as a selfish bitch who was betraying their sisterhood. D'neen, worried if she decided to go along with the kidnapping, what would Charles think of her, if her role was ever discovered.

"What are you going to do?" Katrina asked.

"We need you," Tasha added.

D'neen remembered how angry she had been at Ashley for trying to seduce Charles. She thought what if it was Charles that had moaned Ashley's name during their love making.

"Okay, I'm in -- we're not going to get caught, are we?"

"Everything is going to go smoothly. In and out like a robbery," Katrina joked.

"You know how many robbers are in jail today?" D'neen reminded the girls.

"We're not doing a robbery," Katrina added.

"How are we going to do it?" D'neen asked.

"First we need you to re-establish your relationship with Ashley Gray." Katrina said.

"What?" D'neen snapped.

"We need information on Ashley's whereabouts and work schedule. It would be best to snatch her when she's not expected to be at work," Katrina instructed.

"What about her boyfriend?" D'neen asked.

"What boyfriend?"

"The guy who spilled the drink on you at the wedding."

Katrina pondered a moment, then said, "Fuck him, we'll work around it. Shit, he'll probably think she's somewhere cheating on him."

The girls giggled.

"We're straight then. D'neen, you handle your part and everything will be fine."

The trio discussed a few more details, then Tasha walked Katrina and D'neen to the door. D'neen walked out first. Afterwards, Katrina turned to Tasha.

"What was it you were about to say before D'neen came over?"

"Uh, I don't know. I don't remember -- I don't think it was anything important."

"You sure?"

"Yeah."

"Alright. I'll call you later."

Katrina left. Tasha walked over to the sofa, laid down, then sighed heavily.

CHAPTER 20

While Ashley sashayed around the radio station, D'neen spied on her from afar. D'neen hated the role given to her in the kidnapping plot. Why was she picked to be the one who had to befriend Ashley, she wondered. But after careful consideration, she had to admit to herself that choosing her made sense. Unlike Tasha and Katrina, her husband did not sleep with Ashley, so there were no permanent scars between her and Ashley. And only she could get close enough to Ashley to get her schedule.

D'neen watched Ashley walk into the ladies' room and figured the time to approach her was at hand. D'neen entered the bathroom and found Ashley drying her hands. Ashley looked at D'neen from the corner of her eye, but pretended not to see her. Ashley awaited D'neen's next move.

"Hello Ashley."

Ashley was surprised by the greeting. She was expecting a sarcastic remark or none at all.

"Hi, D'neen," Ashley said hesitantly.

"About the thing with Charles..."

"I don't have time for your little bullshit," Ashley said heading towards the door.

"Don't leave!" D'neen ordered.

The tone of D'neen's voice caused Ashley to pause, however, D'neen walked over to her submissively, hoping not to trigger any aggression from Ashley.

"I'm not trying to rehash a dead issue. Please hear me out. You and I were once friends, until I got a little out of line when I did the show," D'neen said penitently.

"I'm listening," Ashley said cockily.

"I just wanted to apologize. We're neighbors; work together and I like working here and don't want anything to affect that."

Ashley felt empowered thinking, this little bitch know what time it is. As Ashley gloated inside she kept a stolid face.

"Okay, all is forgiven."

D'neen smiled with relief, but inside she was flaming, "Do you want to do something this weekend?" D'neen managed without being sarcastic.

Ashley thought for a moment, then said, "No, I might go out of town for a few days."

"With that cute guy from the wedding?"

"Karl? No, I'm thinking about giving him some time off. He's getting a little to close. Now he wants to divorce his wife and marry me," Ashley boasted.

D'neen nodded her head smiling, but she was thinking, whatever happens to you, you deserve it, you nefarious bitch.

"I'll see you around," D'neen said, then left.

Ashley was about to leave as well but her stomach churned. She rushed over to the stall and vomited in the toilet.

"Shit!"

CHAPTER 21

When Katrina entered the Tattoo shop, the first thing she noticed was the many artistic designs on the walls. One particular design grasped her attention; it was a black bleeding heart with a hatchet lodged in the center of it. As Katrina stared at the design, she thought, this is what Lewis and Ashley Gray have done to my heart.

"You like that?" The tattooer asked.

The tattooer was a biker type sporting baggy jeans, wife beater, and Timberland boots. His massive chest, neck, arms, and hands were riddled with tattoos.

Though she had heard the question, Katrina didn't immediately turn to face the tattooer standing behind her because she was crying inside and wanted her moment. When she did turn around and laid eyes on the guy, her first thought was, I could hire this guy to scare the shit out of Ashley or do something far worse.

"What's up pretty?" The tattooer said flatteringly.

"I want to get a tattoo."

"The art you were staring at?"

"No, something simple, personal -- The word revenge."

"Ouch. I'd hate to be on the other side of your vengeance."

The tattooer looked Katrina over admiringly, thinking she's too sweet to hurt anyone. Little did he know? Katrina knew what the guy was thinking and offered, "Looks can be deceiving."

"You're right, because I'm a big Teddy Bear myself."

As Katrina sat bracing for the tattoo to be written on her shoulder, she stared at the tattoo gun and asked, "Will it hurt?"

"Naw, my hand is soft as your eyes."

"No pain," Katrina said disappointedly.

The tattooer took notice of Katrina's seemingly disappointment. With a sinister smile he offered, "I can make it hurt if you like?"

"No, I was just wondering -- Is it difficult to tattoo someone?"

"Well I'm an artist, but you have a lot of amateurs out there doing shitty work. Why, you want to start tattooing?"

"No, just making small talk."

After getting her tattoo "Revenge" on her shoulder, and engaging in further conversation with the tattooer, Katrina left. She drove to a backstreet, turned her car off, and waited. Ten minutes later she glanced at her watch impatiently. She was about to start her ignition when someone tapped on the window. Katrina smiled.

A tall sleek looking man with piercing eyes opened the car door and settled into the passenger's seat. He leaned over and kissed Katrina on her cheek.

"Hey girl."

"You're fifteen minutes late," Katrina said with a sly grin.

"I haven't seen you in three years and this is how you greet me?"

"How are you doing Torey?"

"The question is how are you doing girl?"

"Me, I'm good."

"I don't know about that."

"Forget the bullshit, did you bring it?"

"What's going on Katrina?"

"Nothing."

"Nothing uh? You call me out of the blue and all you say is meet you here and you need to borrow a gun."

"Did you bring it or not? Katrina said trying not to sound impatient as she was.

"Yes, but why do you need a gun?"

Katrina looked relieved, "Nothing is going on. I'm going to start working late hours and I wanted some protection until my background check clears."

"Why didn't Lewis get you protection?"

"Come on detective. Hand it to me."

Torey paused for a second, then reached into his waistband and removed a 38 revolver. He reluctantly handed it to Katrina who studied the gun for a moment.

"It's cute."

Torey scoffed, "Guns aren't cute -- Katrina don't give me back a gun with a body on it."

"Who am I going to shoot? I just want to feel safe when I'm on the street."

"Okay -- have you seen Ashley lately?"

"I see her now and then."

"What are you doing later?" Torey gave Katrina a look with his piercing eyes.

"You know I'm married."

"I'm just saying, what's dinner between friends?"

"Then what, you banging me? Torey, I don't cheat."

"You take care of yourself -- I'm always here for you."

"I know."

Torey leaned over and kissed Katrina on her cheek then exited the car. Katrina studied the gun again and placed it under her seat and drove off.

CHAPTER 22

At the hospital, Tasha exited the ER and walked down the corridor then stopped in front of a female nurse. While they engaged in a friendly conversation, Vern eased up from behind Tasha and kissed her on the cheek. The kiss surprised the nurse who knew both Tasha and Vern but never suspected that there was something going on between them. Tasha turned around angrily believing it was Bruce.

"What the hell!" Tasha snapped.

When she saw that it was Vern she didn't lose her anger, but she did gain another emotion, which was embarrassment. Tasha cut her eye at the nurse who pretended not to be surprised by the kiss, but Tasha knew better. The nurse just gave Tasha a warm smile. Tasha hated that smile. It was the kind of smile that said everyone in the hospital will hear about this.

"You left this at my house," Vern said.

Vern extended his arm to hand the earring he was holding to Tasha, who folded her arms across her chest and stared at the earring as if it was a snake.

"That's not mine," Tasha said awkwardly.

"Tasha, I'll see you later," The nurse said, giving Vern a smirk before walking away. When the nurse was out of sight, Tasha poked Vern in his chest with a stern finger.

"What the fuck is wrong with you?

"Why are you snapping at me?"

"Are you trying to be smart?"

"I thought it was your earring?"

"Give me my damn earring," Tasha said as she snatched the earring from Vern's hand.

"I want to apologize for kicking you out my house. When you threw up on me, I lost it."

"No need to apologize."

"I want to see you again."

Tasha scoffed as she turned to leave. Vern reached out and grabbed her arm, stopping her. Tasha looked at Vern's hand on her arm then glared into his eyes, Vern released his hand promptly.

"I really want to see you again."

"For what? You got what you wanted, right?"

"I got what I wanted? You came to my house 4 o'clock in the morning. I think we both got what we wanted? But it's not about that, I like you," Vern said in a softer tone.

Vern touched Tasha's chin softly with the back of his hand, "Let's start over with dinner?"

Just as Vern removed his hand, Tasha saw Bruce approaching from behind Vern. When Bruce came near, he gave Vern a quick look over then turned his attention to Tasha.

"Baby, can we talk?"

"What are you doing here Bruce?"

"Excuse us," Bruce ordered, rather than asked Vern.

Before Vern could render a verbal response or physical reaction, Bruce audaciously stepped between Vern and Tasha, with his back to Vern. Vern, who was several inches shorter than Bruce, looked at the back of Bruce with disdain. Vern's ego suffered a blow. He had never suffered such disrespect, especially in front of a woman. He placed his hand on Bruce's shoulder.

"Excuse me," Vern said sternly.

Bruce turned around looking annoyed, "Leave me alone right now, I'm talking to my wife."

Vern chuckled. It was the kind of chuckle that a man

gives another man suggesting that he slept with his lady. Bruce felt it, and it hurt. "I said I'm talking to my wife, walk away," Bruce said turning to face Tasha.

Again, Vern felt disrespected as he stared at Bruce's back. Repeating the same scenario, Vern placed his hand upon Bruce's shoulder. Bruce responded by catching Vern in the jaw with the back of his right hand, a classic bitch-slap. It wasn't a devastating blow, but it had the intended effect. Bruce had sized up Vern when he first approached and knew it wouldn't take much to dismember him.

Bruce's second blow was a straight right hand to the center of Vern's chest, taking away his breath. Bruce then negotiated a technique that had Vern sprawled out on the floor and Bruce kneeling over him with his hand clamped around Vern's Adam's apple. The entire assault was clean and professionally done, taking no more than a few seconds.

As Tasha watched, she was surprised and amazed at the skills Bruce displayed. She had never known that he could handle himself so well in a fight. While Bruce stood over Vern like the alpha male wolf over an inferior member of the pack, Tasha was turned on by the sight of his strength. But when she noticed the other spectators also watching the incident disappointingly, she came to her senses and yelled, "Bruce stop it, stop it."

Bruce had blacked out. It took him a moment to hear Tasha's voice screaming at him to do something. He turned his head slowly towards her. His movement, which looked more mechanical than human, along with his blank stare, scared the shit out of Tasha.

As Bruce released his victim, he saw the fear in Tasha's eyes and shook his combat mode. But Tasha was still afraid. When she saw security quickly approaching she felt a little safer.

"Are you fucking him?" Bruce yelled.

"No," Tasha said meekly.

Vern finally made it too his feet. Security went to

apprehend Bruce, but Vern said, "Wait, nothing happened here, just a misunderstanding."

Security paused. Bruce glared at Tasha, then walked away. Tasha rushed over to Vern and pulled him close by his arm.

"Are you okay?"

Vern snatched his arm away, gave Tasha an unpleasant look, then walked away. As the spectators dispersed, Tasha just stood there muddled. For the first time in her life she saw another side of Bruce and it scared her.

CHAPTER 23

Although Ashley felt nauseous, and craved a hot bowl of chicken soup and a cool bed, she decided to do her show anyway. She had hoped by toying with a few pathetic callers she might feel better. But her first caller, a religious fanatic, annoyed her with his persistent condemnation of Ashley and everyone else who had ever fornicated or even entertained the thought of it. Before Ashley clicked the caller off she got him to admit that he had had sexual affairs with women at his church, but he claimed to have seen the errors of his ways beginning two days earlier.

Ashley's current caller, an articulate gentleman with an authoritative voice, was a formidable opponent. His series of personal questions were beginning to get underneath Ashley's skin and it showed on her face. If only her audience could see it.

"And what makes you so intelligent?" Ashley chided.

"My intellect or lack thereof, is of no significance to your listeners. What everyone wants to know is why do you hide your frailty behind this image of a strong, independent, sexually uninhibited woman."

"You don't know a thing about me?"

"Were you loved as a child?"

"What are you a psychologist?" Ashley said irritatingly.

"Did I touch a nerve?"

"You wish you could touch something on me."

The caller chuckled, "There you go alluding to sex, or trying to hide behind it. What's your reason for doing this?"

Ashley hesitated to respond. She knew the caller was right, but she wasn't about to admit to him, or her devoted listeners. She would continue to deal with her demons in her own way.

Ashley brainstormed for witty responses, but none was forthcoming. So she did the next best thing to save face, she went to a commercial. As Ashley sat there sizzling with anger, her cell phone rang. She looked at the number, it was her mother. Ashley sighed and let the call go to her voicemail. Moments later Ashley clicked on a new caller.

"Ashley?" The female caller said in a pleasant voice.

From the sound of the caller's voice, Ashley assumed this caller would be friendly. She was relieved, welcoming a break between the verbal sparring.

"Hey, what's going on sweetie?"

"Are you in love with my husband?" The woman asked harshly. Ashley was jolted. Any other day she would welcome this kind of dialogue, but today she was too stressed out to listen and respond to a squawking jealous wife. Ashley was about to hang up, then she thought this could be interesting.

"Who said I know of anyone by the name of Karl?"

"I never said his name, but for the record, his name is Karl."

"Is it Karl with a C or a K?"

"You sleep with a married man and don't even know which consonant he begins his name with?"

Oh, a smart bitch huh, Ashley thought as she perked up. "If this caller's name is Sherri, the one who lays around the house all day doing nothing, yes I'm sleeping with your husband. And for the record, my man spells his name with a K, but I guess you know that because he is in fact your husband," Ashley said empathically.

"Why are you so mean?"

"Why are you so pathetic?"

"We have a family -- Do you know we have children?"

"Who cares?"

"You are nothing but a whore. Karl uses you, he doesn't care about you. Karl cares about me and the kids."

"I'll tell you what, after Karl divorces your sorry butt, I'll allow the kids to stay at my place on Sundays. And to show you I'm not as inconsiderate as you think I am, I'm going to allow your two brats to call me mommy."

"Something bad is going to happen to you."

"Are you threatening me?"

"No -- people like you always get what they deserve."

"Listen Sherri, Karl told me that you snore like a motorcycle. Sleeping with you was like sleeping with a stick. And your breath stinks, that's why he doesn't kiss you."

Ashley paused and waited for a response, but she could hear Sherri sobbing in the phone. Ashley looked sorry as she cleared her throat.

"I have some advice for you. Don't confront the woman, check your man. When Karl eventually walks out on you, get a makeover, step your game up, and maybe you'll meet someone that can put up with your sorry behind."

Before Sherri could respond, Ashley disconnected the call. Ashley had initially tried to be considerate but she couldn't resist the opportunity to berate a weeping wife on the air.

***

Sherri's hands trembled uncontrollably. Her marriage had been in trouble long before Ashley came along, but this was the first confrontation with a woman Karl had cheated with, and it was devastating—the last straw.

Sherri stood in her living room and looked around the

room at so many memories. She picked up her wedding photo taken fifteen years earlier. After staring at the photo she laid it down on its face.

Sherri then made her way to her bedroom. It was once a place of love making and happiness, now it was a place of loneliness and sadness. She looked to the ceiling thinking about something. When her mind was satisfied, she removed a pill vial from the dresser drawer, and dumped the entire bottle of pills in her mouth. Before she swallowed a single pill, she lost the nerve to take her life. She spat the pills into her hand, tossed them into the wastebasket, then laid on her bed in a fetal position and sobbed.

***

Back at the radio station, Ashley walked out of her studio. The entire station was quiet, with every eye on Ashley. The staff had heard Ashley chew into wives and girlfriends on her show repeatedly, but this time it was different. It was as if Ashley had crossed the line. The atmosphere was thick with discontent and Ashley felt it. But she pretended not to notice the discontent on the faces of the staff as she waltzed through the station and out the door into the parking lot. Once she sat behind the wheel of her car, her stomach churned. She opened the door quickly and vomited outside the car.

***

Meanwhile, back at Karl's place, he entered his bedroom and found a sobbing Sherri lying on the bed.

"What's wrong with you?" Karl asked uncaringly.

"Out of all the women you could have cheated with, you picked a witch. Do you even realize that you're sleeping with someone evil and incapable of human emotions? What's wrong with you, are you doing drugs."

Although Sherri had no doubts that Karl was sleeping with Ashley, she was hoping that he would deny it. She figured that if he denied the affair the marriage could somehow recover from the lies. But silence meant he was ready to move on. Karl was silent, Sherri knew how the night would end. Karl wondered how Sherri had found out about Ashley. But he was happy that she finally knew so everything could be brought out into the open. Now they could make a clean break.

"I'll gather my things now. I'm going to make sure you and the children are taken care of. I'll continue to pay your car note."

"Thank you, I appreciate it," Sherri said calmly.

"I never intended this."

"Some things are just not meant to be—we just grew apart."

As Karl packed his things, he occasionally cut his eyes over to Sherri who sat Indian-style on the bed. She had dried her eyes, and surprisingly, looked better.

"Well I'll give you a call tomorrow, I'm sorry – I'll send the divorce papers by in a few days."

"Okay. Karl, you take care of yourself," Sherri said nodding with a slight grin.

"You too."

Karl kissed Sherri on her cheek. Although she was calm about the breakup, Karl wasn't buying it. He was expecting a hard slap across the face, but all he got was a soft touch on his cheek by Sherri. Karl was relieved that things weren't messy. For a second, he attributed Sherri's calmness to the possibility that she herself was cheating. He dismissed the notion and gave her a look of goodbye. Karl turned for the door. Before he could leave, Sherri hurled a glass at him that crashed into the back of his head cutting him.

"Aaaah!"

Before Karl knew what hit him, Sherri was upon him with a hammer. He turned just in time to arrest her wrist in mid air, preventing her from pounding him. As Karl wrestled the hammer free from Sherri's hand, he saw rage and pure hatred in her eyes.

"You want to kill me now!" Karl yelled at Sherri in disbelief.

"Get the fuck out! Go be with that radio whore! She's probably fucking every damn guy that listens to her show! Get the fuck out bitch! I hate you! Fuck your mother too!"

Karl shook his head pitifully at Sherri, then left. As he walked down the stairs, he looked up and saw his children standing in their doorway looking down at him. He was too ashamed to say anything to them, so he left the house hoping that he had done the right thing.

***

Across town Katrina had listened to Ashley's castigation of Sherri. It was one thing for the mistress to admit to sleeping with your man, but when the torment is heard in the homes of thousands of listeners, she was going beyond the call of duty.

"Welcome to the club," Katrina said just above whisper. Katrina picked up her pocketbook and walked down into the basement. She removed the 38 from her pocketbook, she looked at the gun and smiled. She opened the cylinder and checked to ensure that the gun was empty. Then with a devilish grin, she pointed the gun at an imaginary figure of Ashley and pulled the trigger.

"Bang, you're dead Ashley Gray."

Katrina tapped something she had in her blouse pocket and said, "Soon baby, real soon."

Katrina looked around the basement for an ideal place to hide the gun. When she found the right place, she secured the gun out of sight. As Katrina walked back up the stairs, she thought about Ashley and what she and her cohorts were about to do to her. Not a speck of doubt entered Katrina's heart about their mission. And after reflecting on Ashley's brutal treatment of Sherri, Katrina felt that their actions toward Ashley were not only necessary, but justified. Katrina even considered tracking down Sherri to see if she wanted to join the team.

CHAPTER 24

Apparently in a hurry, Ashley rifled through her purse as she walked briskly into the supermarket. More concerned with what she was looking for and not paying attention to what or who was in front of her, Ashley collided harmlessly into a woman who was exiting the market.

While the two women exchanged pleasant apologies, the woman's warm expression melted away as she squinted when she looked at Ashley with a sense of familiarity. Ashley brushed aside the woman's look and proceeded into the market. The woman watched Ashley for a moment then walked into the parking lot.

Ashley made her way to the pharmacy section, stopping in front of a shelf containing items for women. She scanned the shelf for a moment, then picked up a home pregnancy test. She then turned to leave but stopped and grabbed an additional pregnancy test from the shelf. After paying for the two tests and leaving the market, Ashley walked through the parking lot towards her car. Halfway there she was approached by the woman who she had bumped into.

"Hi. Excuse me, but you look familiar," The woman said politely.

Ashley paused with caution. She was accustomed to being accosted by disgruntled wives or girlfriends. This compelled her to be on her guard at all times. Since the woman exhibited no signs of hostility, Ashley lowered her guard.

"I don't think we've met before," Ashley said searching the woman face for recognition.

"Are you sure, because you look so familiar?" The woman said being polite and docile.

"I don't forget faces, sorry," Ashley said confidently.

"I'm certain you're the stinking bitch that slept with my boyfriend."

As the pictures of many men flashed through Ashley's mind like a flickering deck of cards, without warning, the woman spat in Ashley's face and hit her over the head with a four-pack of D-batteries she had just purchased from the market. Ashley dropped the plastic bag with the two pregnancy tests. Ashley was dazed as she dropped to one knee. When the cobwebs cleared some, she patted her head checking for blood. The blow, though heavy, didn't break the skin. Ashley gathered herself and stood erect as she looked around for witnesses. There were several onlookers yards away but none had interfered with the assault or attempted to stop the woman from fleeing into the night.

Ashley picked up her bag and hurried to her car. When she reached her car she cursed and shook her head staring at a slashed front tire.

"Fucking weak bitch."

Ten minutes later Ashley thanked the guy who had changed her tire. With intentions of not calling, Ashley took her helper's number that he offered. She then hopped in her car and sped off. When she arrived home she went straight to the bathroom and looked into the mirror checking for a bruise or cut from the blow she had taken. Satisfied that there was no physical damage, she opened the pregnancy test.

Ashley wasn't a big fan of faith, but as she peed on the stem of the test she prayed that her stomach problems were the results of some kind of bug and not because a baby was growing inside of her. She placed the test on the sink, sat on the edge of the tub and waited. Minutes later, with her heart racing, she looked at the test and smiled halfheartedly when she saw the plus sign signaling that she was with child.

"Shit!"

Ashley went over to the sink and splashed cold water on her face. She had mixed feelings inside. She snatched the other test from the bag, but she couldn't pee. It took her twenty minutes to go, and when she was ready to pee, she repeated the same ritual and waited, only to get the same results.

"Damn!"

Ashley sighed heavily then she sat on the closed toilet seat. She rubbed her stomach and thought, how did this happen? Then she chuckled recalling how it did happened, but with whom she wasn't sure.

This was Ashley's second pregnancy. The first one ended in an abortion when she was fourteen. Not because she wanted to abort her child, but because of the circumstances, her mother felt it was no other choice. It was a family secret that must die with the child, Ashley's mother had told her. Since that day, Ashley hated her mother.

Ashley's thoughts drifted back many years earlier when her world was much different. She had gotten pregnant by a man she dubbed a monster, who happened to be married to her mother. The monster not only stole her youth, he, along with Ashley's mother, who ignored the abuse, was the reason Ashley had lost her ability to love and care for others. When she needed someone, there was no one there for her and she blamed the world and all those in it.

Ashley wiped away a tear and shook her head, erasing the hurt of the past from her immediate thoughts. She forced herself to concentrate on the here-and-now. Ashley laid out in her mind a things-to-do-list for the following morning. First she would visit her doctor to confirm the pregnancy. Next, depending on the results, she would make a decision whether or not to keep the baby and act accordingly. Finally, she would get a reference to a therapist to finally help her deal with the issues from the past and the present. Ashley's thoughts then moved to the potential fathers. They were Bruce, Karl, and Lewis, and though she viewed the chances as slim, she couldn't discount the one night stand from the club. She had taken him home and put the condom on him herself, but what really gave Ashley her doubts was that during intercourse she stopped him before he ejaculated and sent him home because of his lack of performance in the bed.

Ashley stood up from the toilet seat, looked at both pregnancy tests, and sighed. She went into her bedroom and changed into a sweat suit and laid across the bed.

Ashley ran down the possible scenarios of dealing with the possible fathers. If it was Lewis, she believed he would probably initially deny that he was the father and probably deny even sleeping with her because of his fear of Katrina. And if Katrina didn't kill Lewis, he would come to his senses and come crawling back to Ashley to be in the child's life.

Ashley believed Bruce would be different. He was a man who would never deny a child. He always talked about his daughter and professed his love for children in general. Ashley smiled thinking about Bruce. But the question she asked herself, would Bruce give her child equal attention as he gave his first?

Next were thoughts of the one night stand. Ashley prayed that he wasn't the father. She couldn't even remember how he looked. Good thing his number was still in her phone.

Finally, she thought of Karl. He had children of his own and loved them very much. He would welcome a child with her, given the fact that he was dying to marry her. Ashley began to paint a portrait of family life with Karl.

For starters the kid would have everything Ashley

didn't have as a child. She would protect the child against a monster like the one she had to contend with. They would eat breakfast and dinner together, with Karl cooking each meal. They would do family vacations and trips to the zoo. Then she wondered if she could really do the family thing.

"Hey baby," Karl said.

Karl's voice nearly scared Ashley into shock because she didn't hear him enter the room. After realizing her heart wouldn't burst from the rapid pumping, she hopped off of the bed and jumped in Karl's face, her own face filled with fury.

"What the fuck are you doing sneaking up on me?"

"I didn't sneak up on you. I simply walked into the room, you were lying there apparently thinking about something important."

Ashley folded her arms across her chest and fixed her eyes on Karl. She saw something in his eyes that suggested to her that he had indeed snuck up on her. He looked back at her questioningly.

"What?" Ashley said beating him to the punch.

"What do you mean what?"

"You sneaked in here unannounced -- you're staring at me as if I did something wrong?"

"What is going on with you?"

Karl embraced Ashley. He held her close and rubbed the back of her hair for a moment. He then guided her to the bed where they sat.

"What's going on baby?"

"Your wife called the station fucking with me. Were you listening?"

"No, I didn't catch it."

"Did you speak with her today?"

"Yes. I told her that it was over for good, I left tonight."

"Did she tell you about our exchange on the radio?"

Karl chuckled, "No, I guess that's why she threw a

glass at me and tried to crack open my head with a hammer."

Ashley thought for a second that the woman who had attacked her could be Karl's wife, then recalled the attacker saying boyfriend not husband, so Ashley didn't feel the need to mention the incident to Karl.

"Are you okay?"

"Yeah, I just have a lot on my mind," Ashley said standing.

Karl reached out and took Ashley's hand in his own, "I love you Ashley."

As Ashley stared down at him she wondered if she could share a life with him. That caused her to remember leaving the pregnancy test in the bathroom out in open view.

"I have to go to the bathroom," Ashley said shooting into the bathroom.

She snatched the tests off the sink, wrapped them in toilet tissue, put them into a plastic bag, and tossed the bag into the wastebasket. She headed to the door and stopped, remembering that sneaky look in Karl's eyes. She removed the plastic bag from the wastebasket, grabbed a towel, and wrapped the towel around the bag and put the towel at the bottom of the clothes hamper. Ashley had heard many stories about snooping men and figured Karl was one of them.

When she walked back into the bedroom Karl was stripped down to his boxers, lying across the bed smiling. Ashley smiled and laid next to him. "I don't want to do anything, can we just talk?"

"Yeah."

Ashley rested her head on Karl's chest enjoying the aroma of the oil based cologne he sported.

"What's on your mind baby?"

"Nothing, I just want to lay here."

Karl's antennas went up. Ashley had just contradicted herself. First she said she wanted to talk, seconds later she just wanted to lay there. Knowing women can be evasive, Karl knew he had to finesse the situation to get Ashley to reveal her thoughts.

"You can talk to me about anything Ashley."

"I can?"

"Of course."

Ashley and Karl laid silent, both of them engulfed in their own thoughts. Ashley was debating whether to reveal that she was pregnant. Karl was hoping Ashley would agree to marry him.

"Did you give any thought to my proposal?"

"What proposal?"

Karl smirked. He knew Ashley was playing mind games so he decided to play along.

"About me moving in."

"What? You never asked to move in?"

"I was talking about marrying me?"

Ashley didn't respond, she just stared at the ceiling wondering would you still want to marry me if I was carrying another man's child.

"Ashley, do you know how to love?"

Ashley wasn't shocked by the question. She had been asked that many nights while lying in the arms of a man. But Karl would receive the same answer all the others received, which was silence.

Realizing that he wasn't going to coax Ashley into a serious conversation, Karl began to caress her breast. She became moist between her legs, but she made up her mind that she was not going to fuck no matter how horny she got. Then Karl stopped his hand motion.

"What's this?" Karl asked squinting.

"What?"

"Give me your hand."

Karl guided Ashley's hand to a tiny lump underneath the skin of her breast.

"You feel that?"

"Yeah."

Ashley sat upright and rubbed across the lump,

"What is it?" Ashley said talking aloud to herself.

"Do you have a history of breast cancer in your family?"

Ashley was stunned hearing the word cancer. She thought about the call she received from her mother stating that she was sick. Ashley thought maybe her mother had cancer and wanted to tell her about it.

"It can't be cancerous, I'm only 30."

"It's possible that a 30 year old woman could have breast cancer."

Ashley looked terrified. Karl saw it and wished he could take back his words, but they were true.

"But it could be a lymph node," Karl said trying to ease Ashley's fears.

"I'll get it checked tomorrow when I go to the doctor."

"Are you sick?"

Ashley stood up, her face angry, "You have to leave."

"Come on with that."

Ashley walked to the door and stood there waiting for Karl to leave.

"I want you out of here!"

Karl looked at Ashley as if she was crazy. She showed no emotion. Karl got up and starting dressing. This was the second woman tonight that was kicking him out. He finished dressing and walked over and kissed Ashley on her cheek.

"Whatever's on your mind I hope you come to terms with it. I'll talk to you in the morning."

"I don't know, I might be going out of town for a few days."

"Where are you going?"

Ashley was about to respond with a smart remark, but Karl looked more concerned than jealous, so she withheld the sarcasm.

"I might go to visit my mother, but I'm not sure. I'll call you if I decide to go."

"Promise?"

"Yes."

Karl kissed Ashley on her cheek then walked into the hallway.

"Karl."

Karl stopped, hoping Ashley had changed her mind.

"Leave your key."

Karl returned to the bedroom, sat the key on the dresser then left without saying a word.

Ashley laid on her bed with a new worry, it was called cancer.

CHAPTER 25

Since D'neen had agreed to participate in the kidnapping of Ashley, she had been edgy and distant. She wondered if Charles was feeling the tension because he had been staying out later, even on work nights. And when D'neen questioned him about the change, Charles simply gave her the line that all men use, "I was having fun with the boys." However, in Charles' defense, it was the truth. D'neen was unfortunately on the fence with whether or not she believed him and this doubt added to her stress, triggering more discomfort to her aura.

On this particular night, D'neen was more restive than usual. She was home alone and bored. Charles had called telling her that he was going to hang out with the boys for about an hour, that was three hours ago. Sitting there staring at her fingernails, D'neen did what many women in her unstable condition would do, she suspected that Charles was seeing another woman. The thought of him making another woman feel as she felt when he touched her was too agonizing. D'neen tried to shake the thought by concentrating on the positive aspects of their marriage.

Restless, and with her mind in a tug-a-war concerning Charles' fidelity, D'neen turned on the television to help her relax. She foolishly settled on watching an episode of Cops. The show featured, as usual, the police on foot chasing down a suspected criminal; slamming him down to the concrete with six cops jumping on the guy's back to subdue him.

Any other night this scene wouldn't have affected D'neen, but tonight the scene and the show triggered thoughts of the crime she was about to commit. Though Katrina and Tasha downplayed the kidnapping as a little fun, comparing it to an in-and-out robbery, D'neen knew the matter was as serious as Hurricane Katrina in New Orleans in 06'. D'neen chuckled thinking Tasha would laugh when she called Katrina, Hurricane Katrina.

D'neen thought about the possibility of something going wrong with the kidnapping. "Nothing's going to go wrong," she heard Katrina's voice whispering in her head. As D'neen watched the police slap handcuffs on the wrist of the criminal on the show, D'neen rubbed her own wrist imagining handcuffs being placed on her if something should go wrong with the kidnapping. She envisioned Hurricane Katrina and Tasha getting away, and she's being left alone to fend charges, with Ashley blaming her for everything.

The thought of going to prison scared D'neen. She turned off the television, laid across the bed, and turned her thoughts back to Charles. She glanced at the clock, it was 11:45 p.m. Once again D'neen thought about Charles with another woman. She tried to shake the thought but couldn't. She picked up the phone to call him but sat it down not wanting to be a nagging wife. Her mother warned her against being a nagging wife.

Ignoring her mother's warning D'neen called Charles anyway, but his phone was off. She couldn't believe it. She called right back but the phone was still off. Now her suspicions were heightened because Charles' cell phone was never off.

D'neen sat down tapping her toes rapidly on the floor. She thought about calling Charles' friends, but was pissed because she didn't have any of their numbers. D'neen went into serious jealous mode. She darted to the clothes hamper, picked up a pair of his underwear, and smelled them. They smelled like Charles. She felt silly but picked up more underwear and smelled them. She couldn't detect any suspicious odors and was surprisingly upset.

D'neen sat on the floor resting her back against the bed. She recalled recent conversations with Charles, searching for any hint of another woman and she came up with nothing. She looked for credit card bills or receipts; there were no suspicious purchases. She rifled through his shirts and pants pockets. By the time she reached the last pair of pants, she was winding down emotionally and feeling foolish, but when she reached into the last pocket and felt a tiny piece of paper, her heart dropped. The paper was too small to be a receipt. It could only be what she dreaded, a phone number. When she removed the paper and looked at it she was correct. It was the phone number Charles had taken from the woman at the mall.

D'neen's hand trembled, her heart-rate increased, her stomach felt empty and her lips went dry when she saw Ashley's name written over the number.

"Motherfucker!"

D'neen stared at the number and shook her head in confusion, "This isn't Ashley's number."

D'neen picked up the phone and dialed Charles. The call when to his voice-mail. She was pissed. She dialed the number on the paper.

"Hello?" The woman on the other end asked.

"Can I speak to Ashley?"

"You have the wrong number," The woman said then hung up.

D'neen felt offended as she called back.

"Hello?"

"Is this 844-2314?"

"You called it?"

"Can I speak to Ashley?"

"You just called here, I told you, you have the wrong number," The woman said then hung up.

D’neen sat there wondering what to do next. As she stared at the number, she assumed that the name Ashley was probably a code name for the woman on the phone. D’neen called the woman back, but the woman didn’t answer. D’neen was livid. She waited five minutes then called back.

“This is the third damn time you called my phone, maybe the person you’re calling had this number before me. It’s after midnight and I have to work in the morning --”

“I found this number in my husband’s pants.”

The women went silent for a moment. “Oooh,” the woman said softly.

“What, why did you say that?”

The woman didn’t respond but D’neen could hear her giggling.

“What are you laughing at, are you fucking Charles? Just tell me. Be a woman and tell me the truth, are you fucking my husband? Did you know he was married?”

“Listen, you have the wrong number. Please don’t call me again.”

“Bitch, are you fucking my husband?”

The woman hung up. D’neen wanted to throw her phone against the wall. But instead she called Charles. Still no answer. D’neen stood up and looked around the room not knowing what to do. She looked at the clock, it was 12:13 a.m. D’neen slipped on a pair of jeans and put on her sneakers. She grabbed her car keys and went and hopped in her car.

As she put the key in the ignition, she paused not knowing where to look for Charles. She got out the car and turned her attention to Ashley’s house. D’neen was about to walk over and knock on the door but came to her senses. She went back inside her house and peered out the window waiting for Charles to come home.

Ten minutes later Charles pulled his car into the driveway. D’neen ran to the door. Without opening the door, she placed her hands on her hips and waited. When Charles opened the door D'neen jumped in his face startling him.

"Who are you fucking? What's her real name? Are you fucking Ashley? Where were you at? You don't love me? You're playing games now? You want to divorce, separate, what?

Charles was speechless. He didn't have a clue as to what D'neen was yapping about. He thought she was rehashing the Ashley thing because he was late coming home. Charles was about to turn around and walk out the door but the pain in D'neen's eyes stopped him.

"Calm down. What is wrong with you?"

D'neen couldn't hear Charles, she was still shooting questions in rapid succession. Charles listened without hearing until he had enough. He walked past D'neen and mounted the stairs. D'neen stood dumbfounded as she watched him walk away from her. To her, his actions translated to an unfaithful man. She raced behind Charles only to fall on the stairs injuring her knee, but she was too upset to feel the pain.

Charles entered the room and undressed to his boxers and t-shirt. Moments later D'neen marched in. She walked over to Charles while he was sitting on the edge of the bed and smelled his t-shirt and his crotch area, shocking Charles.

"What is wrong with you?"

"Who are you sleeping with? Were you with her tonight? Just tell me yes or no," D'neen said in a calm voice, as she searched his pants pockets.

"I am not cheating, I was out with my boys."

"Why was your phone off?"

"I didn't realize it was off."

D'neen didn't buy the excuse but accepted it. Holding the smoking gun evidence in her hand, she waited for the right moment to spring it on Charles.

"Where did you go tonight?"

"We went --"

Before Charles could finish, D'neen handed him the

phone number, with an I-busted-you look on her face.

"Whose number is this?" D'neen asked.

"I don't know."

"You don't know?"

"A woman at the mall gave me the number. The only reason I took it was because I thought Ashley put the woman up to it."

As D'neen listened to Charles relate what happened at the mall, she thought this is all bullshit.

"Call her."

"No."

"Call her, you got something to hide?"

"No. I'm tired, we're not going to talk about this. Throw the number in the trash. D'neen, I'm not cheating on you, if you believe that I am. I don't know what to tell you but I'm not. I'm going to sleep."

"Oh, it's like that?"

"It's nothing to talk about --Maybe you're doing something, you been acting funny around here lately."

D'neen was stunned that Charles was now accusing her of being unfaithful. She was about to go off but something settled inside of her. She told herself, if Charles is cheating she would soon learn for sure, so she decided to just wait. She removed her clothes and laid next to him.

"I swear to God that I will never hurt you D'neen."

D'neen didn't respond, she just laid there quietly.

"My mother is coming to stay with us for a couple of weeks and I don't want her to see us fighting about nothing."

"Your mother is coming here?"

"Yes."

Before D'neen fell asleep, she thought her marriage was falling apart and she blamed Ashley. There were never any problems until Ashley tried to seduce Charles. D'neen made up her mind that she wasn't going to back out on the kidnapping.

CHAPTER 26

Friday, 6:10 a.m. Katrina awoke with a sinister smile and a look of mischief in her sparkling eyes. She felt energetic and strong, as if she had the power to conquer the world with her two skinny hands. For a moment she watched Lewis sleeping peacefully next to her. She quietly got out of bed without awaking him and went into the bathroom.

As Katrina showered, her emotions were erratic because this was the day that she, Tasha, and D'neen planned to kidnap Ashley. Though the intended abduction was hours away, the anticipation of it had Katrina so anxious she broke out in hives. An adrenaline rush stifled the itchiness she would've otherwise felt.

After showering and dressing in a pair of sky blue Capri pants, a pink button down shirt, and pair of Nike track sneakers, Katrina did something she hadn't done since before Lewis had cheated with Ashley, she cooked breakfast. Cinnamon French toast and beef sausages.

Lewis awoke while Katrina was in the kitchen. As he walked into the hallway and headed towards the bathroom, he stopped when the aroma of the sausages cooking in the kitchen tingled his nose. It was a smell Lewis wasn't used to, at least in his home. He turned around and walked back into the bedroom and sat on the edge of the bed wondering why Katrina was cooking. He glanced at the clock and saw that it was 6:52 a.m. Lewis raised a suspicious eyebrow then proceeded back toward the bathroom.

After Lewis bathed and dressed, he walked into the kitchen and found Katrina in front of the stove fully dressed. Lewis stood in place and watched Katrina oddly. The entire scene was wrong; Katrina fully dressed at seven in the morning, in front of the stove cooking. He noticed that she did look sporty.

"Good morning baby, sit down," Katrina said without turning around.

Lewis stared at Katrina a moment, then complied. Katrina could feel Lewis' staring eyes burning a hole in her back and she loved it. She let him sit there for exactly three minutes musing over her actions. Katrina then walked over and sat a plate in front of him. She surprised Lewis by kissing him in the mouth. It was a hard, lascivious kiss with a lot of tongue. Lewis was dazed. He couldn't recall Katrina ever kissing in that manner.

After the kiss, Katrina got a plate of food for herself and sat across from a stunned Lewis. She smiled and moved her eyes from Lewis' eyes to his plate suggesting that he eat his food. Lewis ignored the food and studied Katrina's eyes which were wide with anticipation, for what, Lewis hadn't a clue. But he was determined to find out.

Katrina's peculiar behavior caused Lewis to believe that she was trying to poison him. He thought back five years earlier when Katrina, with a smile on her face and calm demeanor, threatened to poison him, then stab him before he died of the poison. Back then Lewis thought it far-fetched that Katrina could do something so devious. But after the Ashley incidents and the years of witnessing Katrina's unpredictable behavior, Lewis knew he couldn't put nothing past her. Lewis was certain that Katrina had found out about his rendezvous with Ashley or maybe the others, but was playing it cool until she was ready to make her move.

"What did I do to deserve breakfast?"

"I just felt like cooking."

Lewis wasn't buying it. He waited for Katrina to eat,

but she didn't touch her food. She seemed to be waiting for him to eat first. Lewis thought the whole thing was something out of a movie when the wife poisons the husband. Katrina smiled at Lewis, knowing that he was probably thinking that she cooked the food with rat poison or something deadlier.

"Why aren't you eating?"

"You first,"

Katrina bit her lip softly with a smile. She then walked over to Lewis and stood at his back with a steak knife in hand. Lewis didn't want to overreact by spinning around and confronting Katrina because he could be wrong about her intent. But he did brace himself for the sharp blade of the knife but it didn't come.

Katrina picked up his fork and with the knife she cut a piece of the sausage and held it to Lewis' mouth. He didn't take the food. Katrina laughed. She nudged Lewis in the back then ate the sausage from the fork.

"I know what you were thinking," Katrina said with a smirk.

"What was I thinking?"

Katrina didn't respond. She sat in her chair and began eating her food, Lewis followed suit.

"You're in a good mood, what's up for today?"

"Life is good -- Did you see my tattoo?"

Katrina didn't wait for a response as she showed Lewis her [revenge] tattoo. He looked at it in disbelief, and then he dropped his fork.

"I wanted something simple."

Lewis stared at his plate thinking, the bitch got me. He was about to make himself vomit.

"You're tripping. You think I poison our food? Now I'm on some murder-suicide shit huh?"

"I have to get ready for my flight."

Lewis walked upstairs into the bedroom followed closely by Katrina. He removed his overnight bag from the closet. Before he could pack anything, Katrina grabbed his toiletries, his underwear, and t-shirts and started packing them. Lewis sat back and watched Katrina as she packed. She had never helped him pack before. And if the cooking was strange behavior, her packing was even stranger. Katrina never liked it when Lewis went away on trips because she figured the trips were both business and pleasure. Now she looked eager to send him on his way.

"All done."

"Thanks-- It feels like you're rushing me out the house."

"I am. I have a couple of guys coming over when you leave."

Lewis didn't find anything funny in Katrina's statement and it showed on his face.

"I'm joking. I can't help my husband?"

Lewis didn't say a word. He grabbed his bags and walked to the door, then stopped. He looked at Katrina with curious eyes. Katrina walked over and kissed him on his cheeks.

"Be careful."

Lewis shook his head then left without responding. He hopped in his car and sat behind the wheel. Before Lewis pulled off, he looked at his house and wondered what Katrina was up to?

Katrina went to the closet and removed a pair of black slacks and a black long sleeve cotton shirt. She placed them both on the bed. Though the clothes were neatly pressed, Katrina rubbed the clothes repeatedly, smoothing them out and thinking tonight is going to be a good night.

CHAPTER 27

Tasha awoke at 8:15 a.m. feeling fantastic because she had slept well. In spite of the fact that she had consumed a considerable amount of alcohol and was only able to catch a few hours of Z's.

Before Tasha could sit upright on the bed, she had to remove Vern's limped arm from over her bare chest. She placed her hand on her forehead and shook her head as she watched Vern who was sound asleep and snoring lightly. Bruce never snored, Tasha reflected.

After Bruce had dismantled Vern at the hospital, Tasha had spent the entire day apologizing to him for Bruce's behavior. Initially Vern was cold towards Tasha, but her persistence prevailed and he accepted her apology on behalf of Bruce.

After their shift was over Tasha and Vern found a bar, downed too many drinks, and ended up at Tasha's place. She was happy that her daughter, along with her nineteen year old niece who was babysitting, were both asleep. Once at the house, it wasn't long before Vern and Tasha staggered into her bedroom.

While Tasha was watching Vern sleep, he awoke. She smiled at him and kissed him softly on his lips. The kiss gave Vern an erection so he rubbed Tasha's inner thigh. She climbed on top of him, straddling him. Tasha leaned forward and kissed Vern on his neck.

"Mommy I want my daddy," Tasha's daughter said

standing in the doorway rubbing her sleepy eyes.

"Shit!" Vern said pushing Tasha off of him.

Vern and the daughter's eyes met. She looked at him strangely as if she was expecting him to be her father. Embarrassed, Vern averted his eyes. Tasha wrapped a sheet around her nude body and rushed over to her daughter.

"What are you doing sneaking in here?" Tasha said in a gruff voice.

Tasha led her daughter by the hand back to her room. Tasha's niece was still asleep.

"Get back in bed baby."

When the daughter climbed in bed, the niece woke up to find Tasha glaring at her.

With the innocence of a child, the daughter asked, "Mommy, that man in your bed wasn't daddy, what was y'all doing?"

The niece looked at Tasha with a grin. Tasha averted her eyes embarrassingly.

"You were supposed to be babysitting."

"I --I, uh--"

"Mommy, why was you sitting on that man?"

The niece could no longer hold the amusement. She laughed out loud. Tasha wracked her brain for a response.

"You were dreaming," The niece said rescuing Tasha.

"Go back to sleep baby."

"I thought I was asleep?"

"We are sleep," Tasha's niece said wrapping her arms around the child.

Tasha glared at her niece again then walked out the room. When she entered her bedroom, Vern was fully dressed and standing in the center of the room.

"I'm going to leave."

"I'm sorry about that."

Tasha slipped on a pair of jeans and a t-shirt then walked Vern to the door.

"I'll call you later," Tasha said.

"I guess she's going to tell her daddy on me?" Vern said with a half-hearted smile.

"It's okay."

Tasha gave Vern a peck on his lips then opened the door. As Vern was leaving, Katrina was entering.

"Who was that, the milkman?"

"Thank God you wasn't Bruce."

Katrina took a seat on the sofa, Tasha stood in front of her.

"Girl, I got a lot to tell you. I'll be right back."

Tasha shot up the stairs and opened her daughter's bedroom door silently and peeked in. Both her daughter and niece were asleep. Tasha went back to the living room and sat across from Katrina.

"So who was the guy?"

"Vern."

"The same Vern you threw up on?" Katrina said surprisingly.

"Yeah."

Tasha then filled Katrina in on the latest. First, she covered the incident that occurred at the hospital. Katrina took interest in the fight asking questions and making hand motions mimicking Bruce's technique from what Tasha demonstrated as she spoke.

Next, Tasha told Katrina about how her daughter walked in on her when she was about to ride Vern. Katrina couldn't help but laugh, but she did apologize to Tasha for laughing.

Katrina related how she had played with Lewis' head, then both women went silent for a moment. Tasha was hoping her daughter would forget the incident. Katrina thought about asking Tasha did she remember what she wanted to say to her a few days ago when D'neen had interrupted. But Katrina decided to drop the matter.

"Are you ready for tonight?" Katrina asked

anxiously.

"Yes. Are you?"

"Can't wait?"

"Have you spoken with D'neen?"

"She should be here in a few minutes."

CHAPTER 28

Ashley awoke at 7:00 a.m. to the sound of her alarm. She rubbed her stomach thinking about the pregnancy. She then moved her hand slowly upward, hoping that the tiny lump on her breast would somehow be gone. Unfortunately, the lump was still there.

The prospect of cancer provoked thoughts of her mother and whatever ailment she was suffering from. Ashley wanted to call her mother and ask questions, but she couldn't bring herself to pick up the phone.

Although Ashley knew it could only be a few minutes after seven, she glanced at the clock anyway, anticipating her doctor's appointment which was a little less than two hours away.

After showering and dressing in a full-length skirt and a button down shirt, Ashley went into the kitchen, made four slices of toast, poured a glass of orange juice, and sat down in front of the plate. However, she didn't touch the toast, she just sat at the table thinking about her mother. After ten minutes of mulling over whether to call, Ashley decided to pick up the phone.

Ashley was adamant that she was calling for her own benefit of finding out if her mother had breast cancer. As she waited for her mother to answer the phone, she had no concern for the welfare of the woman who gave birth to her. After four rings, Ashley clenched her teeth when she heard her mother Lisa's voice.

"Hello?"

"Lisa, this is Ashley, Ashley Gray," Ashley said sternly.

"I know who you are. How are you doing baby?"

"I'm just calling because you called me --What's wrong with you?"

"I heard you on the radio several times, you sound good. I'm happy that you are doing so well."

"You are sick, right? What do you have?"

"Cancer," Lisa said bravely.

"Cancer?" Ashley said weakly.

"Yes, cancer."

There was silence. The word cancer was stuck in Ashley's throat like a golf ball. She thought about the possibility of having cancer herself and the chances of dying from it. As Ashley thought about her demise, something happened within her. From the tenderest place in her heart, where a speck of compassion was somehow able to survive amidst the pain, hurt, and coldness, Ashley felt sympathy for her mother, and it surprised her.

"What kind of cancer do you have?"

"Breast cancer."

"What are you taking?"

"Well, the damn chemo took all my pretty hair. I wear a wig now -- You know you got your long beautiful hair from me. Is you hair still long?"

"Yeah."

Ashley heard murmuring in the background. She was about to hang up after having expressed some form of kindness and concern for her mother.

"Hey Ashley, how are you doing?" The stepfather said with a chuckle.

His voice shot through Ashley's vein like a tranquilizer made up of something evil. Ashley froze with fear. Although she was hundreds of miles away, in the safety of her own home, the man on the other end of the phone still terrified her. His voice was raucous and his words were counterfeit. Ashley couldn't imagine this man caring one bit about how she was doing.

Ashley's mind told her, do not listen to anything he had to say, hang up. But Ashley's hands disobeyed the order. As her stepfather continued to speak pleasantries, Ashley's mind drifted back in time.

Ashley had a flashback, she was thirteen years old. She thought she was home alone with her mother and stepfather both at work. Ashley was in her bedroom stripped down to her panties and bra, she was dancing in the mirror to a rap video on the television. Imitating the video girls, Ashley made her butt bounce to the music, that's when her stepfather entered her bedroom. She stopped dancing immediately and told him to leave. On two prior occasions when he had entered her bedroom, he complied with her orders, but tonight he didn't. And judging from how he stared at her; like no grown man should look at a girl her age, Ashley knew what he was thinking. She screamed for her mother to rescue her and prayed to God that something would stop her stepfather from raping her. But there was no intervention. Ashley never forgot the pain she felt when he forced himself inside of her both physically and mentally.

"Ashley, I heard you're doing real well with that radio thing."

The stepfather's voice brought Ashley back to reality, but she didn't respond. She was still frozen, but not with fear, hate had replaced it. Ashley could hear her stepfather tell her mother in the background that he didn't think she wanted to talk.

"Ashley, are you there? I love you," Lisa said.

"Bitch you don't love me! You love a monster!"

"I know a lot of things happened in the past, but John was drinking back then. Now he's sober."

"Alcohol didn't rape me and get me pregnant, your

fucking monster did!"

"Please don't call him a monster? He changed -- he -- he's working now as a counselor for troubled youths."

"What! He won't be working there tomorrow. I promise you that!"

"Please don't cause trouble."

"Trouble! Monsters don't change, especially without punishment. Do you hear me?"

"That was a long time ago, I just want us to be a family again. John is a good man, he helps me, he's sorry."

Ashley laughed, "The monster never said he was sorry to me, and if he did apologize I wouldn't forgive him."

Ashley could hear her stepfather ask for the phone and her mother whispering no. She could also hear what sounded like a struggle for the phone.

"You're damn right I don't want to talk to you motherfucker!"

"Ashley, I need you. I'm sick --"

"Bitch, I don't care let the monster take care of you and don't ever call my phone again."

Ashley hung up the phone and stared blankly at the refrigerator in front of her, but she didn't see it. Her mind was too cluttered with hatred.

CHAPTER 29

D'neen was awakened at 7:30 a.m. by Charles who was stirring about getting ready for work. Her heart rate was pumped up a notch, for this was the morning of the kidnapping and her nerves were uneasy.

D'neen wondered what would become of their relationship if things should go afoul with the kidnapping and she fell into the hands of the law. She couldn't imagine being locked away in some tiny filthy prison cell and picturing another woman's hands and fingernails digging into Charles' V-shaped back while he was deep inside of her. Especially, if that woman was Ashley. D'neen shook her head thinking that scenario would never play out if she could help it.

Under the guise of sleep, D'neen observed Charles silently. He had on a pair of slacks, no shirt, and was barefoot. She studied his movement carefully. Tracing his muscles with her eyes, messaging his back with her thoughts. Looking at his bare feet, with the veins protruding with each step he took, turned her on more. D'neen giggled, amazed at how something so insignificant could arouse her. She recalled her mother saying that when a woman's in love with a man she loves every fiber of his body, from his toenails to the texture of his hair.

Charles felt he was being watched and turned to face D'neen. His initial thought was that she was about to renew the argument about him coming home late. But she remained silent. When Charles and D'neen's eyes met they stared at each other like they did on the day they first fell in love. Their gaze was so strong it was as if they were children playing a game of stare-down, neither wanting to be the first to turn away.

Charles moved to the bed. Though their passion for each other was raging, they made love slow and tenderly. D'neen made love as if this would be the last time in her life to share a moment with Charles. He returned his love so fervidly, making a statement that D'neen understood that his love was for her and her only. It was during that joining of their hearts, minds, bodies, and souls that their first child was conceived.

"I love you baby. I have to shower and get out of here," Charles said as he climbed out of bed.

"Okay -- I might be out late with a couple of my girlfriends."

"Have a good time."

Charles kissed D'neen then went into the shower. After Charles left for work, D'neen showered then dressed in a black sweat suit. She looked at herself in the mirror and saw a woman who had never committed a crime in her life on the threshold of becoming a criminal.

***

Katrina and Tasha sat in Katrina's car in the parking lot at Home Depot. After five minutes of waiting, D'neen drove up and parked next to Katrina. The trio got out of their cars. Katrina looked D'neen over and nodded approvingly of her black sweat suit. D'neen had taken notice of Katrina's black outfit as well. Tasha had yet to dress in her black-on-black get-up.

"I see you're ready," Katrina said.

"You too," D'neen responded.

"Have you spoken with Ashley today?" Tasha directed to D'neen.

"No. I'll see her at work later."

"Okay, I didn't get the handcuffs. We're going to need duct tape and plastic tie-wraps. I saw a steel cable we can attach to her leg --"

D'neen looked around nervously, believing Katrina was talking too loud, "Let's just go inside and get what we need?"

"Okay."

As the women approached the door, a man opened the door for them. The man was Karl, he smiled at the women with recognition. Katrina and Tasha smiled back at Karl recognizing him as well. D'neen recognized him also but turned away from him.

Once inside, Karl spoke to Katrina, "Hi, I'm sorry again about the drink."

"Don't mention it."

"You two were at the wedding as well?"

"Unfortunately," Tasha responded.

"Well, ladies have a good day."

"Do you think you can help us shop, we might need a man to carry something for us," Katrina said surprising both Tasha and D'neen.

"I can give you a hand."

"We can manage ourselves, thank you?" Tasha said.

"Are you sure?"

"Yes," Tasha said cutting her eye at Katrina.

"Have you spoken with Ashley lately?" Katrina asked.

D'neen looked like she would die. Karl himself was also caught off guard.

"Uh--"

"Never mind, we'll see you around," Katrina said smiling at Karl then grinning at D'neen.

Karl nodded to the women then walked away.

"What is wrong with you?" D'neen snapped.

"What did I do?"

"This is a sign. We can't go through with it," D'neen protested.

"Don't be ridiculous," Katrina countered.

"What were you trying to prove by talking to him?" D'neen asked.

"I was thinking maybe we should kidnap him too. After all, he is sleeping with the enemy."

D'neen stared at Katrina in disbelief, "Are you crazy? What if he tells Ashley he saw us together?"

"So what?"

"This is wrong."

Katrina stepped to D'neen, "So once again you're ready to back out on your friends?"

Stepping away from Katrina, D'neen said annoyingly, "Let's just get the things we need and get the hell out of here?"

CHAPTER 30

Ashley sat impatiently in the reception area at her doctor's office. Her face was tensed and her hands were folded resting uncomfortably on her lap. For the fourth time in less than a minute she glanced at her watch, it was 9:20 a.m. She had been waiting since 8:45. The woman sitting next to Ashley smiled at her understandingly. Ashley returned the gesture with a smile of her own. But her smile belied the fear harboring inside of her.

"I used to always be in a hurry," The woman said looking straight ahead as if she was talking to herself.

Ashley's initial thought was to remain silent, letting the statement go duly noted rather than striking up a meaningless conversation with a stranger. But when Ashley noticed the woman was wearing an unfashionable looking wig, Ashley figured the woman could use some fashion tips.

"I'm always in a hurry, but that doesn't stop me from looking my best when I walk out the door," Ashley said hoping the woman caught her drift.

"I know what you mean, but since I've been fighting cancer, I don't have time for trivial things."

Ashley looked embarrassed and stunned, she just stared at the woman with her mouth agape. The woman looked back at her impassively causing Ashley to look away in shame.

"I'm sorry," Ashley said staring at the floor.

"You have nothing to be sorry about, it's not your

fault. Cancer is like a bad man. It just appears out of no where to fuck up your life just when things are going well."

The woman laughed. Ashley tried to hold in her own laughter but couldn't. After the two shared a laugh, Ashley wanted to wrap her arms around the woman and tell her, I feel you sister. But that wasn't Ashley's style so she just asked, "Do you mind me asking, what type of cancer do you have?"

"Breast cancer."

The woman related how she first felt fullness in one of her breast, then pain, redness, and a discharge from her nipple. She promptly made an appointment for a radiologist and after going through a series of examinations, she was diagnosed with stage 1 breast cancer.

The woman removed her wig and rubbed her bald head proudly. Ashley was astonished at the woman's bravery to flaunt her clean round head whose hair had succumbed to chemotherapy. From that moment, the woman's bald head would be etched in Ashley's mind her entire life. Ashley pictured herself being bald, the thought of it made her sick.

The woman whipped out a photo of herself before the hair loss. She had beautiful auburn hair. Her face was fuller and her eyes were happier. The woman's before-and-now transformation was too much for Ashley. Again, Ashley wanted to share her fears of having cancer with the woman, but she couldn't open up to share.

Five minutes later Ashley sat in the examination room waiting for the doctor to return. She had taken a pregnancy test but she didn't inform the doctor of the tiny lump on her right breast. She wanted to wait to find out if she was in fact pregnant, which she already knew was the case, but her mind was in disarray, affecting her sense of judgment.

The doctor entered the room smiling, "Ashley, you're going to have a baby," handing her a prescription for prenatal vitamins.

Ashley didn't share his happiness. Her mind was on the possibility of having cancer. The doctor noticed Ashley's lack of enthusiasm and lost his joyful look.

"There are options."

"I have this tiny lump on my breast. It's not really a lump, more like a tiny bump," Ashley said in a dry voice.

"Are you experiencing any fullness, redness, and discharge?"

"No."

"Is the lump movable?"

"I believe so. Yes it's movable."

Putting on a pair of latex gloves, the doctor said, "It could be a cyst, fibro adenoma, adenomas, or papillomas."

"I'm too young for cancer? What about the baby?"

"Let's make sure we know what's going on before we jump to conclusions. It could just be one of the lumps I mentioned."

"Of course," Ashley said trying to sound optimistic.

"Ashley, can you open you blouse?"

The doctor proceeded to conduct a physical examination on Ashley. He began with her left breast. Ashley was told to raise her left arm. With the flat surface of his fingers he applied light pressure by depressing the surface of the skin, feeling for tiny lumps near the surface. He then pressed deeply into the tissue. Next he used the spiral method to check the breast, he detected nothing. He repeated the same method on the right breast and discovered the tiny lump.

"Here it is. It's movable."

"Is it cancer?"

"Like I said, it could be a cyst."

When the doctor mentioned the need for additional tests, Ashley's mind was foggy. She barely could hear the doctor as he explained the need for a mammogram, blood and urine test, and fiber optic scope and biopsy. By the time the doctor mentioned something about surgically removing a tissue sample from the possible malignancy and studying it under a microscope to check for cancer cells, Ashley was drunk with terminology.

"What about the baby?"

"Well…"

"Can I have a fucking healthy baby or what?"

"It is possible to have a healthy baby, but there are always risks. Since the lump is movable I'm leaning towards it being something benign. I want to do a mammography today and schedule an appointment for Monday morning with my good friend, who is an Oncologist. I want to also sign you up for a comprehensive program of prenatal care with a specialist. We're going to takes things one step at a time."

After Ashley's mammography, the doctor studied the image encouragingly, "I'm encouraged by what I see."

"Good."

"But like I said, we're going to do more tests on Monday."

Ashley looked frazzled. The room felt like it was slowly closing in on her.

"I need some time to think. This is too much for me right now, I'll see you on Monday."

While the doctor was in the middle of advising Ashley, she stood up from her chair and left the office, walking out into the warm afternoon air. The doctor rushed to the door and stood in the doorway yelling out to Ashley to come back to his office, but she continued to walk comatose-like, then breaking into a jog towards her car. As she sat behind the wheel of her parked car, she began to sob.

She thought about the baby. She wondered if she did have cancer, would the kid have a chance. Having an abortion crossed her mind and the thought of it hurt. It also brought back memories of her mother.

Ashley smacked her palm against the steering wheel.

"Damn."

"Are you okay?" A passerby said, leaning close to Ashley's window.

Ashley was startled by the intrusion. She stared at the guy for a moment without speaking. He saw her tears and waited for a response. Ashley didn't know whether to yell at the guy for intervening in her moment or to lie to him by saying she was okay. She settled for the middle ground by saying, "There is no problem here."

The guy reluctantly walked away, but not before taking one last look back at Ashley. When he was out of sight, Ashley touched the tiny lump on her breast, something she had been doing since she had discovered it. Ashley wanted to talk to someone, a friend to confide in. She thought about who should she call. After a minute of thought, the only person she considered close enough to be a friend was Karl. But she didn't need a man, she needed a woman who would understand her dilemma. Then it hit her. At that moment she realized she was completely alone in the world.

Ashley started her ignition, but didn't know where to go. She thought about going to work, but dismissed the thought because work would probably only make her more stressed out than she already was. Then Ashley shocked herself by picking up her cell phone, and with great pain, she called her mother and told her that she would stop by for a couple minutes tomorrow night.

Ten minutes later Ashley found herself sitting in a sports bar. She almost ordered alcohol, but caught herself thinking about the baby.

As Ashley sat nursing an orange juice, within a span of twenty minutes she had been hit on by four men. Each leaving with a feeling that the beautiful woman was one not to be messed with. Ashley was about to leave, when a guy at least ten years her junior sat next to her.

"How are you doing?"

Ashley sighed, "Can I ask you a question baby?"

"You can ask me anything with those sweet lips."

"How old are you?"

"Twenty."

"Do you find me attractive?"

"You are beautiful. That's why I came over to speak with you."

"Now be honest. Would you stick your dick or tongue in a vagina filled with radiation?"

"What?"

"I said would you stick your dick or tongue in a vagina filled with radiation?"

"I don't know what the fuck you're into, but you can take that somewhere else."

The man gave Ashley a look, and like the four men before him, he walked away whispering something under his breath. Ashley chuckled thinking that sooner or later she was going to come across a man who would say, "Yes, that's what condoms are for." Ashley left the bar and decided to stop by the radio station, but not for the purpose of working. The station was the only place she felt at home and she wanted to be around people, even if they didn't particularly care for her.

CHAPTER 31

At 7:30 p.m. Tasha and Katrina entered Tasha's house. Katrina carried a black knapsack over her shoulder and Tasha was carrying a shopping bag from a clothing store. Both women looked tired, but they still walked with zeal. They had spent the day securing a safe place where they could hold Ashley. The place they chose was a small cabin twenty minutes away from the city. The cabin and location was ideal for what the girls had in mind. They also rented a vehicle for the transport and traveled the route two times just to make sure there wouldn't be any problems with traffic or the road.

Everything was in order and ready—no problems, except for a close call at the hospital when Vern had walked in on Tasha as she was swiping anesthesia and syringes. To divert his attention away from the stolen items she held behind her back, Tasha kissed Vern on his lips, and whispered in his ear, promising that something freaky was going to happen to him the next time they had sex. As Vern backed out of the room smiling, Tasha finally realized after forty years on Earth that when it came to sex men were easily distracted and open for manipulation. At that moment, Tasha felt foolish for having endured Bruce's bullshit for so many years; all along she had the power of persuasion between her legs and didn't realize it.

"I have to change," Tasha said.

Katrina sat on the sofa and rested the knapsack on the

floor next to her. She leaned her head back and closed her eyes. She wondered if her cohorts realized how serious of an undertaking they were about to embark on. To Tasha it seemed to be a big game, but D'neen was visibly shaken whenever the word "kidnap" was mentioned. Katrina giggled thinking that D'neen was so square that every time she had sex the lights probably had to be turned off and she had to do it under the covers.

Katrina opened her eyes and scanned the room, not focusing on anything particular, but a framed picture sitting on the mantel grasped her attention. She walked over to the mantel and removed the photo of Tasha's daughter when the child was an infant. Katrina stared at the picture with a strange interest. Moments later her eyes became watery, her lips tightened, and the muscles in her face tensed with anger. She sighed, then looked upward engulfed in a thought. As her mind drifted to another time and place, Tasha entered the room; her presence brought Katrina back to the here-and-now.

"I see you're looking at my beautiful baby girl," Tasha said without paying close attention to Katrina's face.

"Yeah, she's beautiful—All babies are beautiful," Katrina said matter-of-factly as she turned away from Tasha to compose herself.

"So how do I look?" Tasha asked.

Katrina turned around and grinned at Tasha who was now clad in all black, and sporting a black silk tie around her neck.

"You look ready to take care of business," Katrina said.

"Thank you."

"Can I use your bathroom?"

"Go ahead. I have to call and check on my daughter."

Katrina picked up her knapsack and walked upstairs to the bathroom. She stared at her face in the medicine cabinet mirror. She noticed how sad her eyes were. She told herself that her eyes would no longer be sad after this weekend. She reached into the knapsack and removed a pair of large scissors and began cutting her hair. When she was finished, her hair was cropped unevenly, but she liked it. She walked back to the living room. When Tasha saw Katrina from across the room, she placed her hand over her mouth in surprise.

"What did you do to your hair? I have to fix it," Tasha said walking over to Katrina.

"No, it's fine. It fits my mood. I'm in warrior mode."

"I see," Tasha said nodding her head.

"I'm going to check on D'neen."

As Katrina picked up her cell phone, Tasha realized that she and Katrina were operating on different pages mentally, but Tasha dismissed Katrina's oddness as pre-kidnapping hype. Oh, how wrong she was.

***

At the radio station D'neen looked nervous and disjoined. Several co-workers had asked if she was feeling well. Each time D'neen lied with a fake smile. D'neen was far from okay. It was only a few hours away from the abduction and her nerves were in shambles.

She glanced at her watch, Ashley was an hour late for work. Tardiness wasn't an attribute of Ashley's and D'neen was beginning to suspect that she wasn't coming in at all. D'neen asked one of the engineers if Ashley had called in, he responded that he hadn't received any calls. Hope began to seep into D'neen's mind that Ashley had left for the trip she was talking about, but just as D'neen's nerves were beginning to settle, she heard Ashley's voice calling out to her.

"Hey Baby Girl."

"Shit," D'neen whispered under her breath.

D'neen turned around and saw Ashley standing behind her. D'neen immediately noticed how stressed

Ashley looked.

"Ashley, are you okay?"

Ashley hesitated a moment. She wanted to tell D'neen about the pregnancy and the possible cancer, but Ashley did what she was accustomed to doing, she lied.

"I was almost in an accident and the guy had the nerve to come on to me. Like I would get with a guy who drives a car for under twenty grand."

D'neen shook her head slowly, "I know what you mean -- You look really tired Ashley."

"Just a little. But a little fatigue doesn't stop a trooper from work."

"Are you still going away this weekend?"

"Tomorrow I'm taking a flight out, but I'll be back Sunday morning. Listen, we'll talk later, I'm running late for my show."

When Ashley walked away, D'neen took out her cell phone and called Katrina, "She's here…Okay, I'm going to meet y'all there." D'neen hung up the phone, gathered her things, then left the building.

Ashley sat in her studio in front of the microphone. She was on the air listening to the caller speak about being pregnant and not being sure who the father of the child was. Ashley was initially going to discontinue the call, but curiosity compelled her to engage the caller.

"How along are you?"

"Two months."

"And you're not sure who's the father?"

"No."

"Are you going to keep the baby?"

"Yes!" The woman said emphatically.

"I'm not suggesting anything by the question. I'm just asking for our listeners."

"I didn't mean to snap. I'm under a lot of pressure."

"That's understandable. How did you get yourself in this situation?"

"It's my husband's fault."

Ashley chuckled, "What? Was he pimping you?"

"No. What happened was this: a woman called his cell, I answered, she said that they were just friends. My husband and I got into a fight about it. I confided in his brother who was staying with us. He said if his brother was cheating on me, he was a fool. One thing lead to another, now I'm seeking your advice."

Ashley didn't respond. She was thinking, I'm the last person to seek advice from, you have two potential fathers, and I have four.

"I have another caller who wants to join in. Caller #2 are you there?"

"I'm here. Hello Ashley," Caller #2 said.

"Hey, what do you have to offer?"

"I just waned to tell the whore --"

"I'm not a whore!"

"Yes you are! You are a smut. You're married and had sex with your husband's brother, that makes you a whore."

"It was a mistake."

"Two plus two equals five is a mistake, you knew what you was doing. And I don't want to hear about no alcohol."

"I wasn't drinking."

"You shouldn't have been."

As Ashley listened to caller #2 berate called #1, it was as if the caller was speaking directly to her. Ashley felt the need to defend caller #1 and herself.

"Wait a second, give the girl a break," Ashley said.

Caller #2 chuckled, "You would come to a whore's rescue, y'all stick together right?"

"Now you picked the wrong one?"

"Shut up! I have the right one. Heck, if you was pregnant, you probably wouldn't know who your child's father was."

"Who are you to judge?" Caller #1 jumped in.

"I know who the father of my children is."

"How many do you have?" Ashley asked.

"It doesn't matter, I know who their father is."

After squabbling with caller #2, Ashley stayed on the air for an hour longer, then left the station and headed home.

CHAPTER 32

Karl's wife Sherri drove her car slowly down Kelly Street reading the addresses that were visible on each home as she passed. She stopped in front of her destination and parked across from Ashley's house which was dark inside. Sherri looked in the back seat at her two children who were sound asleep. Watching the children in their peaceful state, she wondered what had possessed her to bring them along. That was the most sensible thought she had all evening.

It all started four hours earlier when Sherri's daughter had asked why was her father moving out. Sherri brought the two children in the living room, sat them down on the sofa and told them: "Your father doesn't love us any more and wants to live with a whore." After feeding the impressionable children with her hate for Karl and not leaving out the obligatory, "Your father ain't shit," statement, Sherri instructed her daughter to ask Karl for the address and phone number where he would be staying in case of an emergency. Just as Sherri was wrapping up with her besmirching of Karl, he entered the house.

Karl spoke to Sherri, but she didn't return his greeting, she walked upstairs to her bedroom. Karl's daughter did as she was instructed and attained Ashley's home phone number and address from her father. When his daughter asked him why he was leaving them to live with a whore, Karl exploded in anger. He raced upstairs and burst into the bedroom. Sherri was sitting on the bed waiting.

"What the hell are you telling those kids?"

"I told them the truth! You're leaving us for a whore!"

An argument ensued. Sherri punched Karl in the face, he countered by slapping her to the floor. Sherri sat there in shock that Karl had put his hands on her. She then jumped up and wrestled with him until they fell on the bed. As Karl pinned Sherri to the bed and yelled at her to calm down, she got aroused and hoped he would have sex with her.

"I love you," Sherri said seductively.

Breathing heavily, she moistened her lips with her tongue. Karl stared at her and shared her thoughts, but he fought the urge to have sex and stood up.

"I'm leaving."

"No! Please don't leave Karl. Come here baby, we can work things out."

Karl stopped and stared at Sherri who was unbuttoning her blouse, "I love you Karl."

"I love you too, but it's over."

Sherri felt like an idiot. She glared at Karl as she fastened her buttons.

"Get the fuck out!"

As Karl gathered the rest of his clothes, Sherri rose to her feet, and without looking at Karl she left the room and gathered the children. But before she left the house with the children, she yelled upstairs to Karl threatening that he will never see his children again.

Now Sherri sat in her parked car across the street from the woman who she blamed for the breakup of her family. She looked in the mirror at the swelling underneath her eye from the slap. "He could've at least fucked me," Sherri thought. She looked at the children again. They were still asleep, her daughter was snoring lightly. Sherri thought about the statement Ashley made on the air about her own snoring. That made Sherri even angrier. She reached under the passenger's seat and removed a baseball bat, then opened the car door slowly.

***

Twenty minutes earlier, Karl sat in his parked car in front of his house. He was hoping that Sherri would bring the children home soon because he didn't want to leave his family in the manner in which he was leaving. He figured she was at her mother's lying on him.

As he waited, he thought about Ashley and why would she take back her key when he didn't do anything wrong. He figured she was just going through something because of the tiny lump on her breast. Karl felt guilty for not telling Ashley that he had gotten a key made the day after she had given him a key. He figured that once he was back in good grace with her, he would tell her about the key just in case she discovered it on her own.

Karl picked up his cell phone and called Ashley but the call went to her voice-mail. He left a message saying that he understood that she wanted the key back, but he believed they could still works things out and that he would stop by in a half hour. Karl hung up the phone, started his car, then headed to Ashley's house.

***

Sherri exited her car holding the baseball bat at her side. She scanned up and down the block; it was dark and quiet. She walked briskly over to Ashley's house, Sherri rang the doorbell a few times, then waited. After a moment, she rang the bell again then knocked on the door. Since no one answered, Sherri hustled back to her car. Hoping not to wake the children, she got in the car quietly, and decided to wait until Ashley came home.

Five minutes later, Karl's car stopped in front of Ashley's house. He hopped out of his car and walked toward the house. He stopped and noticed that two trash cans were blocking the entrance to the driveway. He thought that was peculiar.

"Karl!" Sherri yelled as she exited her car.

Karl was shocked as he saw her approaching him with a bat.

"What the fuck are you doing?"

"You live with this bitch!"

Sherri swung the bat, Karl caught it in mid air. He had to overpower Sherri to wrestle the bat out of her hands.

"Have you lost your fucking mind?"

"No, motherfucker you lost your mind!"

As they screamed at each other, a light from a neighbor's house came on. Karl knew it was a matter of time before the police would be called and he would probably be the one hauled off to jail.

"Get in your car and go home!"

"No! I want to see this bitch!"

"Mom!" The daughter yelled standing next to the car.

Karl saw his daughter then looked at his wife in disbelief, "You got my kids out here in this nonsense."

Karl marched over to Sherri's car. His crying son jumped into his arms. Sherri came running behind him.

"If you don't get my children home, I'm taking them with me. You're going to lose custody when we go to court."

Sherri thought for a moment, then ordered the children back into her car.

"If you don't come back to the house so we can settle this tonight I'm not going anywhere."

Karl knew it was bullshit, they had already settled things. To move the drama away from in front of Ashley's house, Karl followed Sherri back home.

Ten minutes later Kelly Street was once again quiet as Ashley drove her car down the block. When she reached her house and was about to turn into her driveway she saw two trash cans blocking the entrance.

"Shit!"

She figured the kids on the block had placed the cans

there as a joke. They had probably gotten everyone on the block with the gag, Ashley thought. But if she was paying attention, she would have noticed that her driveway was the only one with cans blocking the entrance. Any other night she would have sensed that something was wrong, but after the day she had, she was tired and unfocused.

Ashley exited her car. After moving the cans she walked back towards her car. Just as she reached the driver's door, a black mini-van with tinted windows sped up and stopped in front of her. Ashley jumped back against her car thinking that the driver stopped to apologize.

Before she could curse out the reckless driver as she intended to do, the side door of the minivan opened. An assailant clad in all black and wearing a ski mask jumped out the minivan and was next to Ashley jamming a metal object against Ashley's ribs. In a gruff voice the assailant whispered, "Scream and you die."

Even if Ashley wasn't warned against screaming, she couldn't because fear had suffocated her voice. Ashley was muscled into the minivan. The assailant seated in the passenger's seat, also wearing a ski mask, jumped out and hopped in Ashley's car and drove away slowly, followed by the minivan.

However, before the minivan drove off, the masked driver hopped in the back and poked Ashley in her arm with a syringe, while the assailant who had apprehended Ashley bound her wrist with plastic tie wraps. The driver hopped back behind the wheel and followed Ashley's car.

The drug injected into Ashley began to take effect. Though it was only one assailant in the back seat with her, Ashley saw four of them. Ashley mumbled something. The assailant reached in the black knapsack and removed a pair of dirty panties and stuffed them into Ashley's mouth, then wrapped a thin scarf around Ashley's face securing the panties in place. Moments later Ashley was unconscious.

The abduction of Ashley took less than forty seconds.

Not a professional kidnapping, but it was efficient. If there were any witnesses, all they could say was that a woman had gotten thrown into a minivan, someone jumped into her car, and they drove away. And the perpetrator had on all black.

Ten minutes later, Ashley's car and the minivan came to a stop outside a parking lot. The assailant driving Ashley's car pulled into the parking lot, parking Ashley's car. The assailant who no longer wore the ski mask was D'neen. She snatched Ashley's cell phone and pocketbook from the passenger's seat. The phone was placed in Ashley's pocketbook. D'neen pocketed Ashley's keys then threw the pocketbook under the passenger's seat. When D'neen opened the car door to leave, Ashley's phone rang. D'neen paused, debating whether to answer the phone. She decided wisely not to. Before D'neen got out of the car, she looked to be sure that no one was watching her. She locked the door and walked quickly to the minivan and hopped in the passenger's seat wiping her brow relieved that she was not stopped by the police while driving Ashley's car.

Tasha, who had removed her mask, drove off. D'neen looked in the back at Ashley's limped body which laid peacefully on the seat. Katrina held her hand firmly on Ashley's shoulder, like a lioness laying its paws upon its prey until she was ready to devour it. D'neen was puzzled as to why Katrina was still wearing her mask.

"She's unconscious, you can take off the mask." D'neen said.

"I'm fine."

Tasha and D'neen exchanged a look. The drive went without further conversation. Twenty minutes later, the minivan entered a wooded area stopping in front of a nondescript wood cabin. Katrina was the first to emerge. Her eyes were wide with anticipation and sparkled in the moonlight. Tasha walked around the minivan and stood next to Katrina. The two women had visited the cabin on prior occasions and weren't the least bit phased by the locale.

On the other hand, D'neen exited the minivan and looked around in amazement. She had to give it to the girls for choosing this place, the area was ideal for anyone wishing to remain out of sight or for three kidnappers to stash away a beautiful woman. There was no nearby traffic from viewing distance. The closest neighbor was ¼ mile away, and the only light was the natural glow from the moon and stars, and the illumination from a light pole a few yards away from the cabin. There were other light poles in the area, but all the lights had been broken on a previous occasion. D'neen attributed the damage to Katrina. While D'neen was caught up in her thoughts and observations, she didn't notice Katrina and Tasha staring at her with concern.

"D'neen, where are you?" Katrina asked.

"I'm here."

"Tasha, check inside," Katrina ordered.

Tasha entered the cabin. A light was turned on. Moments later, Tasha walked back over to Katrina and D'neen looking satisfied.

"Let's get her inside." Katrina said.

The three women struggled with Ashley's lifeless body as they carried her into the cabin. The cabin was a one roomer; dilapidated, no furniture save a small bed, a wooden table, and four chairs in the kitchen area.

"Lay her here on the floor," Katrina said.

"Why not lay her on the bed instead of the dirty floor?" D'neen asked.

"I said, on the floor."

They laid Ashley down carefully on her back. Katrina removed the scarf from Ashley's face and the panties from her mouth. Katrina reached into her back pocket, and removed a fold out knife and cut the tie wraps from Ashley's wrist. Katrina then hurried out the cabin to the minivan. She returned moments later carrying the black knapsack and a camcorder.

"What do we do now?" D'neen asked.

Katrina didn't respond. She sat the knapsack and camcorder on the floor then removed her mask, finally to D'neen's comfort. D'neen looked shocked to see Katrina's new hair-do. But D'neen didn't comment.

In a move that surprised both Tasha and D'neen, Katrina began to strip Ashley down to her red Victoria Secret panties and bra.

"What are you doing?" D'neen asked.

Katrina ignored D'neen. Unfazed by D'neen's growing irritation, Katrina looked focused as she ordered both Tasha and D'neen to sit Ashley upright and hold her steady. Like the good soldier she was, Tasha followed Katrina's order without question or hesitation and raised Ashley from her left side. D'neen reluctantly lifted Ashley from the right. Katrina dug into the knapsack, out came the scissors.

"What are you doing Katrina?" D'neen asked forcefully.

"I'm giving the bitch a makeover."

Katrina cropped Ashley's hair short then reached into the knapsack. Out came the electric clippers. She trimmed the remaining hair off of Ashley, rendering her completely bald.

"This is extreme," D'neen protested.

"Hair grows back," Tasha offered.

"We didn't agree to this," D'neen countered.

"We didn't agree for Ashley to fuck me and Tasha's husbands. However, we did agree that we would teach this bitch a lesson. Now lay her back on the floor, and turn her face down."

Tasha and D'neen laid Ashley on the floor and awaited Katrina's next move.

"How long before she awakes?" Katrina asked.

"Maybe twenty minutes," Tasha responded.

"Katrina, what are you going to do now?" D'neen asked.

"Can I work without the questions?"

D'neen shook her head slowly looking more irritated. As Katrina removed Ashley's panties, D'neen and Tasha were stunned, but neither said a word. Tasha stared at Ashley's well toned legs and curvaceous ass admiringly, then with jealousy. Katrina reached into the knapsack. Out came the ink and tattoo gun.

"What is that?" D'neen asked.

"A tattoo gun," Tasha responded.

Katrina sat on the floor next to Ashley ready to give her a tattoo, but Katrina looked uncomfortable, she stood abruptly.

"Help me get her on the bed."

The women laid Ashley on the bed face down. Again Tasha stared at Ashley's legs and ass. Tasha wished that she had a body like Ashley's.

"Tasha, get the camcorder and record this."

Katrina put on her mask. Tasha picked up the camcorder and focused the lens on Katrina as she sat next to Ashley and began with the left butt cheek. She tattooed the word "TRASH"; she then moved to the right cheek. D'neen looked uncomfortable as she folded then unfolded her arms.

"I can't watch this."

D'neen walked over to the table, sat down and placed her hand on her forehead wishing she was home. She glanced at her watch. It was 10:30 p.m.

After Katrina tattooed the word "WHORE" on Ashley's right butt cheek, she stood up and folded her arms across her chest admiring her work.

"D'neen, bring me her panties, the ones she was wearing," Katrina said without turning away from Ashley.

"I'm not touching her panties."

Katrina retrieved the panties herself and slipped them on Ashley. Katrina walked over to the metal cable apparatus that was bolted to the wall. She pulled the retractable cable the six feet needed to reach Ashley.

"Tasha, lock the cable in place."

Tasha hustled over to the apparatus, locking the cable in place to prevent any additional slack. Katrina locked the cable around Ashley's ankle.

"Tasha, get the camcorder and put on your mask. D'neen put on your mask and come over here. It's almost time."

Tasha followed the order without pause. D'neen hesitated intentionally before following Katrina's order. Katrina took notice of D'neen's attitude and gave her a look. The trio stood at Ashley's bedside waiting for Ashley to awaken.

"Was it necessary to tattoo her?" D'neen asked.

"What's wrong with branding the bitch?" Tasha asked.

"The tattoo was punitive damages. Punitive damages are always necessary to teach a party a lesson. Now be quiet before she awakes."

Five minutes later Tasha turned on the camcorder and focused on Ashley. Ashley blinked her eyes rapidly as she focused on the masked trio standing before her. Ashley was impassive as she stared at the girls. It seemed that Ashley believed that she was in a dream because it took her a moment to panic.

"Oh my God," Ashley uttered, then fainted.

The trio looked at each other questionably.

"D'neen, get a cup of water."

"Where are the cups?"

"Back at your house. Get a damn cup of water!"

D'neen took offense at being screamed at like a child, but she didn't challenge. She got the water and handed it to Katrina. Katrina shook Ashley by the shoulder. When Ashley opened her eyes, Katrina splashed her in the face with the water. Ashley curled up in fear against the wall.

"Please don't hurt me! Please don't hurt me!"

The tears spilled down Ashley's cheek. Her entire

body trembled uncontrollably. The trio remained silent as they watched. Ashley was so distraught that she didn't recognize that the individuals standing before her were women, she believed her kidnappers were men.

Tasha enjoyed watching Ashley cry through the lens of the camcorder. And of course Katrina loved to see Ashley squirm in fear. It took every ounce of her strength to prevent her from bursting into laughter at Ashley's discomfort. However, D'neen didn't share her counterpart's joy.

"Whatever you want I will give you. I have money. And I can get more," Ashley yammered.

Ashley suddenly realized that she was stripped to her panties and bra. She gasped with a new fear that she may have been raped while she was unconscious. The tears came harder. She prayed that whoever raped her, if she was raped, used a condom.

"I have money, whatever you ask I'll pay. Let me go please. I don't know who you are. I won't go to the police."

After a couple minutes of pleading and offering money, Ashley stopped trembling and gained a little composure believing her abduction had to be about a ransom. Her kidnappers must have believed that she was rich, Ashley thought. She went to touch her hair and realized it was gone. She rubbed her head frantically.

"What happened to my hair? Where is my hair? Oh my God. My hair, my hair!" Ashley screamed.

Katrina retrieved a compact mirror from the knapsack and handed it to Ashley. Ashley stared at her bald head in shock. She thought about the tiny lump, cancer, and the woman at the doctor's office who had lost her hair during her fight with cancer. As adrenaline and cortisone was released into Ashley's bloodstream, her hands trembled. She dropped the mirror to the bed. Her heart rate quickened, her breathing became rapid, her muscles tensed. In her mind she sensed doom.

Tasha and Katrina both knew from the visible

symptoms that Ashley displayed that she was having an anxiety attack. Tasha did nothing but continue to film. For some reason, Katrina believed that slapping Ashley would help, so she stepped forward and slapped Ashley hard across the face.

"Katrina!" D'neen blared out.

Katrina's eyes went from stunned to angry in a matter of seconds. Over the past week she had instructed D'neen and Tasha that no names were to be mentioned during the kidnapping, and if it was necessary to speak, it was to be done in a gruff voice.

D'neen lowered her head regretfully, cursing under her breath. She had broken the glass in a hundred pieces and it was no way to repair it. It would be no walking away from the kidnapping with clean hands. No continuing with life as usual and she would only have herself to blame for revealing Katrina's identity.

But like any optimist in a desperate situation, D'neen had a smidgen of hope that Ashley, in her traumatic state, had missed hearing Katrina's name. Unfortunately, D'neen's hopes were shattered when Ashley leaned forward studying the frames and eyes of the women in front of her.

"D'neen -- Katrina is that you? What are y'all doing?" D'neen turned away in shame. Not Katrina. She stared back at Ashley defiantly. Ashley turned her attention to Tasha, looking at her questioningly.

"Who are you?" Ashley asked pointing a weak finger at Tasha.

"Shut the fuck up bitch," Katrina said in a calm and dangerous voice as she removed her mask.

Tasha followed suit. D'neen also removed her mask, reluctantly. It took Ashley a moment to make out that Tasha was Bruce's wife.

"I don't know what y'all plan was, but it's over. Now let me out this nonsense. Are y'all dizzy bitches crazy?"

"Outside!" Katrina ordered.

As the women walked toward the door, Ashley yelled obscenities at them. She called them everything from dick-eaters to cursing their mothers. Even though the women wanted to return the insults, they held their tongues and exited the cabin. Ashley picked up the mirror and looked at her bald head again, she snapped with a loud grunt. She yanked the cable violently in a desperate attempt to free herself, but the cable was strong. She did nothing more than hurt her hands and tire out.

Once outside, Katrina poked D'neen in her chest. D'neen pushed Katrina's hands away.

"What is your problem?" D'neen complained.

"Bitch, how many times did I say, no names, no fucking names! You don't realize what you did, do you?"

"I know I fucked up," D'neen said walking away from Katrina.

"Take it easy Katrina," Tasha said looking at an emotionally wounded D'neen.

"This bitch fucked up, Tasha."

"D'neen knows."

Katrina kicked a rock angrily, folded her arms, then tapped her toe impatiently to the ground. D'neen wasn't going to let Katrina beat her down with blame. She was also fed up with being called a bitch by Katrina so D'neen copped an attitude herself.

"We can't let her go," Katrina said matter-of-factly.

Tasha and D'neen's eyes widened as they looked at each other. They shared the same thought; Katrina was referring to crossing a line and they weren't going to follow her. Katrina glared at Tasha and D'neen. But it was all an act, because Katrina wasn't mad at all. She was glad that D'neen had lead to the outing of their identities.

Unbeknownst to the other women, Katrina had a deeper reason for wanting to hurt Ashley, and thanks to a slip of the tongue, she had her excuse to get rid of Ashley for good.

"What are you saying, we murder Ashley?" D'neen asked just above a whisper

"All I'm saying is, because of you D'neen we can't let he go."

"I can't be part of a murder Katrina," Tasha said.

Katrina didn't respond. She turned her back to the women and stared out into the dark woods smiling. Tasha and D'neen both watched, wondering what was going on in her mind. Like a submissive puppy, D'neen walked over to Katrina.

"I'm sorry I called out your name, but you slapped her."

"I had to calm her down, she was having an anxiety attack. Tasha, you're a nurse, was she having an anxiety attack?"

"It looked like--"

"That's water under the bridge, we have a major decision to make, because I'm not going to jail," Katrina interrupted.

"We can pay Ashley not to go to the police," D'neen suggested.

"Yeah," Tasha said.

"Do y'all honestly believe if we let that bitch go she won't go to the police?"

"We won't know unless we try," D'neen said.

"Try what bitch? What are we going to do, say Ashley we're sorry, here's a thousand dollars don't tell on us?"

Each time she was referred to as a bitch, the anger in D'neen's eyes grew. Tasha saw it and placed a consoling hand on D'neen's shoulder to ease her tension. Katrina was oblivious to the fire brewing in D'neen.

"What other choice do we have?" asked Tasha.

"Whatever happens, you have this bitch to thank for yelling out my name. I warned, no names."

"Please stop referring to me as a bitch. I don't call

you out of your name Katrina."

Katrina gave D'neen a look, "Oh, I'm sorry. Tasha this B-I-T-C-H --"

"Damn! I knew I shouldn't have agreed to get involved with your crazy ass plan." D'neen snapped.

"Who the fuck are you calling crazy?" Katrina asked with attitude.

"This whole thing is crazy. Renting a van to kidnap someone. Putting panties in Ashley's mouth. What about the drugging, the hair cutting, tattooing a person's butt, that's some crazy shit."

"Did you just curse at me?" Katrina asked obviously looking for a fight.

"You went too far with that crazy ass shit."

"I didn't go too far yet."

Katrina walked up to D'neen and without warning slapped her across the face. D'neen was dazed. Not from impact of the blow, but by the mere fact that Katrina had struck her. D'neen shoved Katrina hard causing her to fall to the ground on her butt. Katrina hopped up charging D'neen. The two women crashed to the ground rolling around before being separated by Tasha.

"What the fuck is wrong with you two?"

"You put your hands on me again and I'm going --" Katrina threatened.

"You're going to do what?"

"D'neen I'm not playing!"

"Don't ever put your hands on me again, because I'm not playing either!"

"We're supposed to be against Ashley but now you two are fighting like cats! Calm the fuck down!"

After a moment of heavy breathing and glaring at each other, Katrina and D'neen calmed down and turned away from one another without uttering a word. Each woman wiped the dirt from their clothing as they were engulfed in their own thought. The ringing of Tasha's cell phone broke the silence.

"Hello?" Tasha said looking worried as she listened to the caller, "Oh no, okay, I'll be there in a half, bye."

"Who was that?" Katrina asked.

"My father. My mother was in an accident, I have to leave."

"What?" D'neen said in disbelief.

"But I don't think I can leave you two alone without y'all killing each other."

Katrina fixed her ghastly eyes on Tasha as her shrewd mind analyzed the situation. On one hand she didn't want Tasha to leave, but on the other she understood. With Tasha's departure, that meant one less person to stop her from tormenting Ashley. D'neen looked like she was struggling with her own thoughts as she glanced at her watch repeatedly.

"If Tasha leaves, I'm riding back with her."

"You can't leave me here alone with Ashley," Katrina said pretending to be upset.

"I didn't tell Charles I was going to be out this late."

Keeping with her act, Katrina rolled her eyes and sucked her teeth, "Okay, you ride home with Tasha, I'll be okay, Ashley is locked up. Y'all can pick me up in the morning."

Katrina was too calm for Tasha and D'neen, they weren't buying it.

"Is that what you want Katrina?" D'neen asked.

"What else are we going to do?" Katrina said as she tried to appear nonchalant about the prospect of being alone with Ashley.

D'neen watched Katrina's face closely and thought it looked devilish under the light of the moon. D'neen knew she had to come up with something or she would have to stay overnight at the cabin with Katrina in order to protect Ashley.

"I got it!" Tasha exclaimed. "We can leave Ashley

here alone until the morning."

D'neen was dumbfounded. She wanted to say the idea of leaving Ashley alone was inconceivable, but she was too stunned to speak. Katrina didn't look happy herself.

"We can't leave Ashley Gray alone. That would be irresponsible. What if someone stumbled upon her here?" Katrina noted.

"Katrina's right," D'neen said.

"No one comes up here, look where we are. Me and Katrina scoped this place out for a couple of weeks," Tasha said confidently.

"I don't know," Katrina said.

"Y'all have a better suggestion? If you do, make it quick, I have to go?"

D'neen thought for a moment then added, "We can drug Ashley like we did before, take her back to her car, and leave. If she wakes up and goes to the police what is she going to say, I've been kidnapped for four hours by three women. We'll deny it. Shit, she might not even go to the cops at all."

Katrina was uneasy as she listened to D'neen's reasoning, which was a good suggestion. But Katrina didn't come this far to walk away without paying Ashley back.

"I agree with Tasha. It wouldn't be a problem to leave Ashley here overnight. After all, she's properly restrained. Tasha has a point, nobody comes out here. It would be good to let her squirm here in the dark," Katrina said.

D'neen weighed the options: leaving Ashley in the hands of Katrina or leaving her alone for a few hours. She chose the lesser of the two evils.

"Okay, she'll spend the night by herself. But we still haven't figured out how we are going to let her go tomorrow."

"We'll figure something out on the ride back to the city," Tasha said heading to the cabin.

Katrina walked over to D'neen and extended her hand, "I want to apologize for slapping you."

D'neen looked at Katrina's hand for a moment then with a forgiving smile, she shook it. Although the women made up, each harbored ill feelings towards each other.

"Shit! Where's the knapsack?" Katrina said.

Katrina took a quick survey of the area then darted into the cabin. She saw the knapsack on the floor where she had left it. She glared at Ashley then rifled through the knapsack and looked relieved that the contents were all there. Tasha and D'neen entered. Without speaking, the trio stood in front of Ashley presenting a united front. But Ashley could see that there was disunity on their faces. Ashley also notice that D'neen's hair was in disarray; and all three of their black outfits still had residue of dirt on them, even though it was apparent that the major dirt had been brushed away.

"Why are y'all clothes dirty?" Ashley's face lit up, "Why were y'all fighting?"

D'neen cut her eye at Katrina. Ashley caught the look and knew that the fight had probably taken place between D'neen and Katrina. "Was the fight about me? You stood up for me D'neen didn't you?"

"Shut up Ashley," Tasha snapped.

"Baby Doll, don't let them force you to do anything you don't want to do."

"Shut up Ashley," D'neen responded.

"No! Take this damn thing from around my ankle!"

"I think it looks good on you," Tasha remarked.

"You have to pay for fucking our husbands --D'neen, get me a pot," Katrina said.

"Your husband? This is about y'all no good husbands. They are the ones who should be chained up. If it wasn't me, it would be someone else. While you dumb bitches are here fooling with me, your husbands are probably fucking someone as we speak. You bitches are so dumb.

Men love to cheat on dumb women. Y'all dumb bitches are going to jail!"

From the looks on the trio's faces, it was apparent that Ashley's words had hurt them. Especially D'neen, who retrieved a pot from under the sink in the kitchen area and handed it to Katrina. Katrina raised the pot in the air threatening to hit Ashley over the head, "I should beat you over your bald head."

"Katrina no!" D'neen screamed.

"I'm just joking. You don't learn, do you D'neen -- Ashley, this is your bathroom."

Katrina sat the pot on the bed next to Ashley who looked at the pot and turned her nose up.

"The choice is yours. Let's go ladies," Katrina said.

The trio turned and walked towards the door.

"Wait, where are y'all going? Y'all can't leave me here! Let me go! I won't go to the police, I promise!"

D'neen was the first to stop at the door. She was desperate to believe Ashley was telling the truth about not going to the police. D'neen reached out and touched Katrina's forearm in a gesture for Katrina to consider Ashley's pleas. Katrina killed D'neen's hopes of ending the ordeal by shaking her head. Ashley looked panicked. She picked up the pot threatening to throw it at the women.

Pointing a stern finger at Ashley, Katrina said, "Throw the pot and not only will I beat you down, you'll have to piss in your panties," Katrina warned as she turned out the lights.

"Good night Ashley," Tasha joked.

As much as Ashley despised peeing in a pot, going in her panties was out of the question, so she sat the pot down on the bed.

"D'neen help me!"

The women left Ashley kicking and screaming on the bed in the dark cabin. As they drove away, D'neen stared back at the cabin until it was out of sight. As Tasha sped down the highway towards the city, she called her father to get an update on her mother. She was pleased to hear the accident wasn't as bad as first thought. She was about to tell the girls the news and turn back, but decided against it.

"Slow down Tasha," Katrina cautioned.

"What are we going to do about Ashley?" D'neen asked.

Neither Tasha nor Katrina had answered. No one said another word until they were back in the city. Tasha parked the minivan on a quiet block where the women had left their cars. It was Katrina's idea to rent the minivan to cut down on the three car traffic driving to and from the cabin.

"We'll meet here at 8 o'clock in the morning. As far as what to do with Ashley, we'll just wing it. If somebody has something in mind, we'll do it. Remember why this thing started in the first place. This is all Ashley's doing, no regrets or backing out," Katrina said looking at D'neen.

"No backing out," D'neen said reluctantly.

The women tapped their fist together then walked to their cars which were parked back to back. Tasha was the first to drive away.

D'neen didn't trust that Katrina was going to drive home rather than drive back to the cabin and do God knows what to Ashley, so D'neen followed behind Katrina to their block.

After they parked and waved goodbye, D'neen waited for Katrina to enter her house before she entered her own. D'neen peeked out the window watching in case Katrina was planning to slip out the house and shoot back to the cabin. Little did D'neen know, Katrina was also watching from across the street in case D'neen was planning on going back to the cabin to free Ashley.

After she was satisfied that Katrina was in for the night, D'neen turned away from the window and sighed. D'neen glanced at her watch. It was 3:18 a.m., she cursed under her breath. Thereafter, she tip-toed up the stairs like a spouse home from a night of infidelity. She crept into the bedroom hoping not to awaken Charles who was sleeping peacefully and snoring lightly. D'neen undressed quietly then crawled soundlessly into bed. A minute later Charles turned over, hitting D'neen with his arm. The contact caused him to awake with D'neen staring into his eyes. Charles' sleepy eyes didn't notice the worried look in D'neen's eyes.

"Hey baby," Charles said groggily.

"Hey," D'neen said feeling busted.

"I tried not to wake you."

"What time is it?"

"It's late."

"Did you have fun?"

D'neen wanted to tell Charles everything that had happened and cry in his arms and listen to his always sound advice. But she held back her problems. She felt too ashamed to reveal the predicament she put herself in. Charles kissed D'neen on the forehead and went back to sleep. D'neen tried to sleep but couldn't. She was convinced that the moment she closed her eyes the police would be kicking down her door like she was America's most wanted; subsequently hauling her out of her house taking her to jail.

Restless, D'neen crawled on top of Charles kissing him softly on his neck and lips. He awoke responding to her advances. Charles began to make love slowly to D'neen, but his passion wasn't enough to erase her thoughts of Ashley locked away in the cabin.

***

Only after D'neen had moved away from her window did Katrina do the same. Katrina turned on the light in the living room and was startled to seeing an angry Lewis sitting on the sofa waiting for her.

"What the fuck!" Katrina said holding her hand over her heart.

Lewis hopped off the sofa and stepped to Katrina

who needed a moment to let her surprise of being startled subside.

"Where have you been?" Lewis yelled.

"Who are you screaming at?"

"Who was you looking at?"

"You were supposed to be out of town!"

"Where the fuck was you at? What happened to your hair?"

"Who are you cursing at?"

"Where were you at?" Lewis said in a calmer voice.

Katrina thought about a lie and was about to respond but hesitated, realizing that for the first time in her marriage she had triggered Lewis' jealousy and it felt good. Katrina decided to play the situation for what it was worth to give Lewis a taste of his own medicine, making him believe that she was out with another man.

"It's late and I'm tired," Katrina said glancing at her watch.

From the furious look on Lewis' face she knew he bit the bait. Katrina headed for the stairs with Lewis following. She swayed her hips as she mounted the stairs knowing Lewis was watching, and he was.

"So you're not going to tell me where you were tonight?"

Katrina stopped in the hallway, looking directly into Lewis' eyes, she said with a slight grin, "I was with the girls."

A feeling of disappointment washed over Lewis. He knew Katrina didn't have any girlfriends so she had to be lying. He gave Katrina a look of frustration then entered the bedroom. Katrina felt sorry for hurting Lewis. She was prepared to soften her stance and reassure him that she had not been unfaithful. But she decided that it was time he felt what she had felt so many nights. Katrina made a detour to the shower. As Lewis assumed she was in the bathroom washing away evidence of cheating, he sat on the edge of the bed debating whether he should leave Katrina tonight. Katrina entered the bedroom wearing a towel. Lewis stared at her curves and was broken-hearted that someone may have enjoyed the pleasures of his wife. At that moment he saw the beauty in Katrina that he had long forgotten. He wondered what had made him stray when he had a queen who adored him.

"Are you fucking somebody Katrina?"

"Are you sleeping around? Because it's odd to ask someone if they're fucking for the sake of asking a question."

"Please answer my question, are you fucking somebody?"

"Is that what you think of me?"

Although Lewis tried to be calm, his frustration was growing with each double-talk answer Katrina gave.

"Are you fucking another man?" Lewis yelled.

"I'm a married woman," Katrina said calmly.

She kissed Lewis on the cheek then climbed in bed. Lewis frowned, remembering all the times he had come home from cheating and gave Katrina an ambiguous answer to her questions. Lewis undressed and climbed in bed next to Katrina. They stared into each other's eyes without blinking. Katrina knew she was hurting Lewis, but she felt no guilt. As she moved close to him, kissing him on the lips. Lewis' first impulse was to push Katrina away, but her forwardness turned him on. As they had sex, Lewis' mind could not erase the thought of Katrina making love to another man. Katrina felt no passion for Lewis and made up her mind that this would be the last time he touched her body. And of course Katrina also thought of Ashley and couldn't wait to inflict more pain upon her.

***

In the pitch black cabin, Ashley sat on the bed thinking, this is some bullshit. Her anger and frustration of being a prisoner replaced her initial fear and uncertainty of being raped, and maybe eventually murdered by her once unknown kidnappers, who she now referred to as the Three Stooges.

Ashley wondered what they had planned for her next. She didn't believe murder was on the table. But in the back of her mind, she knew she couldn't put anything past Katrina. There was too much bad blood between them.

Ashley did take solace knowing that D'neen would never agree to partake in her murder. But what if D'neen wasn't around? The question entered Ashley's mind. Suddenly, a chill swept over her body as she stared into the darkness in the direction of the door. Katrina could barge in at any moment and just kill her, Ashley acknowledged to herself, dreading that possibility. Fear and uncertainty regained their place in Ashley's heart and mind, paralyzing her body and clogging her thoughts.

Ashley sat still in the dark wishing for a flicker of light, because to her light was a sign of hope, and darkness was a sign of gloom. She was a slave to the unknown and was powerless to do anything about it. Ashley rubbed her bald head, remembering the possibility of having cancer. She chuckled, almost hysterically wondered if she would miss her doctor's appointment on Monday. She thought about the pregnancy, and for the first time she considered getting an abortion if she made it out alive.

Ashley told herself that she wasn't going to survive. "How could they let me go, knowing that I will go to the police? But I won't necessarily go to the police," she argued with herself. Ashley's mind drifted to a dire state. She couldn't understand how the Three Stooges could blame her and not their own cheating husbands for ruining their marriage. Why did she taunt those women on the air, she chastised herself. "And who's going to do my show?"

The flood of tears came along with the sniffles, followed by giggling and a shortness of breath. Ashley realized she was a couple giggles away from losing it so she stood up to get her blood stirring and attempt an escape. Unfortunately, her movement was restricted to six feet of slack that the cable provided, which wasn't long enough to reach the door or the two windows that were boarded up. Ashley stood in the darkness like a mannequin deciding what she could do to help herself.

When she realized that the only thing she could do was try to remain strong, she sat back on the bed, sitting on the compact mirror that Katrina had gave her earlier. How she wished for a flicker light, that spark of hope. But as the darkness persisted, the dab of hope she did have faded away as did the minutes, which felt like hours.

Out of the blue, Ashley picked up the mirror wishing she could see herself. Angry that she couldn't see herself, and aggravated with her plight. Ashley had a thought that scared her. She tried to think about something else but the thought kept coming back: She could break the mirror, slice her wrist, and all her troubles would disappear as the blood leaked from her wrist. Ashley hated herself for her moment of weakness. She clenched the mirror then hurled it across the room. Ashley then laid down and sobbed, that's when she felt pain on her butt from the tattoo.

CHAPTER 33

Karl awoke at 6:00 a.m. when he nearly fell off of the sofa as he turned over. He had only gotten three hours of sleep after a night of arguing, crying, and finally reaching an understanding with Sherri. The breakthrough came when she told Karl that, yes, she was very much in love with him, but she loved herself and the children more and she wouldn't allow them to live in a hurtful situation. Knowing that a woman's emotions frequently change like the direction of the wind, Karl decided that it would be best to sleep on the sofa just in case Sherri changed her mind and wanted to drive back to Ashley's house and start trouble.

Karl sat up, placing his face in his hands, thinking about the decision he had made for better or worse. He grabbed his cell phone and dialed Ashley, only to get her voice-mail. Karl hung up the phone, showered, kissed the children goodbye, then headed for Ashley's house.

***

On the other side of town, Lewis awoke to find Katrina fully dressed and standing in the doorway looking at him with a blankness in her eyes.

"Are you going somewhere?" Lewis asked.

"Yes."

"Where?"

"Out."

Lewis shook his head, chuckling slowly as he thought this bitch is getting real cocky. It was too early for an argument, he resigned to the fact that Katrina was seeing someone else.

"How are we doing?" Lewis asked.

"What do you mean?"

"Our marriage."

"Didn't we have sex last night?"

Lewis didn't answer the question. He thought about the many times he had sex with Katrina then had sex with Ashley or someone else hours later.

"I guess you're coming home late again?"

"Yep."

Before Lewis could respond, Katrina's cell phone rang. She looked at the number, smiled, then glanced at Lewis with mischievous eyes before walking down the hallway. Lewis cursed as he pounded the bed twice with the side of his fist.

Next door, D'neen and Charles were both fully dressed, sitting at the kitchen table finishing breakfast.

"What do you have planned for today?" Charles asked.

"Me, Katrina, and her friend Tasha are just going to do some girl stuff."

"Like what?" Charles asked casually.

"I haven't done anything since I moved here," D'neen said defensively.

"Baby, I'm not questioning you, I just asked because my mother will be flying in later."

"I'm sorry."

"You have a good day, I'll see you later."

Charles kissed D'neen on the cheek then left. D'neen cursed. She had to figure out a way to leave the girls at the cabin and come back home. She grabbed her cell phone and dialed Katrina.

Karl parked his car at the curb in front of Ashley's

house and got out. When he saw that the trash cans that were blocking the driveway last night had been removed, he assumed that Ashley was home even though her car was not parked outside.

Karl rang Ashley's doorbell a few times and waited. Moments later he knocked on the door. When no one answered, he reached in his pocket pulling out the spare key. Just then, D'neen exited her house. Karl looked over at D'neen and waved to her. D'neen pretended not to see him as she lowered her head and hopped in her car. Karl jogged over to her.

"Hi," Karl said.

"Hello."

"Have you seen your neighbor?"

"No…but she was talking about going away for the weekend."

"Oh yeah?"

"Yeah."

"Did she say where she was going?"

D'neen gave Karl a look. Karl felt embarrassed, like a teenage boy trying to track down his girlfriend by calling everyone in her family.

"I have to go. Excuse me."

"If you run into Ashley could you tell her that I'm looking for her?" Karl said stepping away from the car.

D'neen pulled off cursing. Karl sat behind the wheel of his car debating whether to enter Ashley's house or drive away.

***

Tasha and D'neen waited outside Tasha's car on the block where the girls parked before taking the minivan to the cabin. Tasha glanced at her watch, it was 7:50 a.m. D'neen filled Tasha in on her encounter with Karl. A few minutes later, Katrina arrived catching the tail end of the story.

"So what, he doesn't know we have Ashley locked

up at the cabin unless you told him," Katrina directed to D'neen.

"Like I would do something like that," D'neen said sharply.

"Kill the in-fighting! Listen, I can't ride up with y'all to the cabin but I'll be up later."

D'neen exhaled, dreading the thought of being alone with Katrina, "I can't stay late."

Katrina sucked her teeth, throwing up her hands in exasperation.

"What's next? Tasha you give me a call, we'll pick you up."

The women tapped their fist together. Tasha hopped in her car and drove away. Katrina and D'neen hopped in the minivan and headed to the cabin.

***

Karl had made up his mind to take a look inside Ashley's house. He got out of his car like a man on a mission, walking briskly toward the house. He inserted the key and pushed the door open slowly. Although he knew he was crossing the line, he convinced himself that he was not doing anything wrong on the premise that Ashley could be hurt inside. Why he thought Ashley was in trouble, he didn't know.

"Ashley!" Karl shouted.

He called out her name a few more times before moving to the kitchen. Everything was in order. He made his way upstairs into the bedroom. For the first time, it occurred to him that Ashley could have been in bed with another man. He was thankful she wasn't.

Karl took out his cell phone and called Ashley. Again he got her voice-mail. He walked over to the dresser and picked up her calendar. He saw the doctor's appointment scheduled for yesterday and thought about the tiny lump on Ashley's breast.

As he sat the calendar back on the dresser, he stared at the closed top drawer; wanting to take a look inside. But he fought the urge, however, unsuccessfully. He knew he was violating Ashley's privacy but he opened the drawer anyway.

There was nothing unusual about the contents in the drawers, a bunch of panties and bras. He picked up a thong, looked at it, then smelled the crotch area. He felt like a pervert so he dropped the thong in the drawer and closed it.

Now Karl's curiosity was worked up. He walked over to the closet, opened the door, and walked inside. Everything was neatly in its place. Of course there were too many shoes from a man's perspective. However, from a woman's advantage point, there weren't enough. Karl admired the expensive dresses hanging from the hangers. He wiped his hand over a couple of them, appreciating their softness. He was about to leave when a small chest caught his eye. He had no business to look inside, but since he had come this far, he said, fuck it.

He opened the chest. The first thing that caught his eye was two pill vials inside of a zip-lock bag. He picked up the bag and read the labels on the vials. The first name was one he could not pronounce, the second was Viagra. He shook his head and looked at the other contents in the chest. Karl's heart skipped a beat when he saw the strap-on dick, the length of which made him feel inadequate as a man.

There were girlie magazines, but he didn't bother looking at them. He picked up a device frowning as he studied it. He wasn't sure of its use, but it appeared to be some kind of device to administer pain. Next was a strap with a plastic ball attached to it. He picked up a plastic bag with different shapes and sizes of vibrators.

Karl was beginning to feel dirty. He then picked up an envelope stuffed with photos of a much younger Ashley in sexual positions with women.

By the time Karl came across the DVDs, he felt

empty inside. As he inserted the first DVD in the player, he braced himself for what he was about to see. The video opened in an average bedroom. Moments later Ashley walked into the frame. She was younger as she appeared on the photos. She blew a kiss at the camera then hopped in bed under the covers. Two guys around Ashley's age walked into the frame. Karl shook his head as he grimaced. The men climbed in bed next to a smiling Ashley.

Karl turned off the DVD and sat on the edge of the bed. He placed his head in his hands in disbelief. A couple minutes later he went to remove the DVD, but curiosity overtook him. He turned back on the DVD and watched a willful Ashley perform in the ménage a trios. Although the video turned Karl on, he could no longer watch the woman he loved in a porno.

He turned off the DVD and replaced it back in the chest; arranging everything as it was before. Karl took one last look at the photo Ashley had of herself on her dresser, then left. As he drove around aimlessly, he wished he had never snooped around in Ashley's house and hoped Sherri would accept him back.

CHAPTER 34

Ashley tossed and turned in her sleep until she finally awoke screaming from several nightmares. In each dream she: defied gravity, ran in slow motion, jumped from one flight of stairs to the next. However, when she jumped, she never reached the floor. In midair she was catapulted into another dream, where once again she was inches away from being murdered by a knife wielding Katrina, only to be saved by D'neen each time.

Ashley sat upright wiping away sweat from her neck and her upper chest. She pulled the sheet from the bed, wrapping it around her shivering body. She looked around the dusty cabin wondering if the Three Stooges had left her there to starve to death.

For the first time since the abduction, she began to observe her surroundings in detail so she could give the police an accurate description of the place where she had been held. Although she had been unconscious during the drive to the cabin, she assumed that the cabin couldn't be too far from the city limits and to the north or west, therefore, it shouldn't be difficult to locate.

As Ashley continued to survey every nook and cranny, she smiled feeling certain that she would be able to lead police back to the cabin, even if she had to search every cabin in the state.

***

Katrina sat impatiently behind the wheel of the minivan at the drive-thru window at McDonalds. D'neen had insisted on stopping to get food for Ashley. After D'neen received and paid for the order, Katrina sped off into the street, nearly causing a three car accident.

"Why are you speeding?" D'neen asked harshly.

"I want to make sure Ashley is still at the cabin."

"Don't you think if she wasn't, we wouldn't be sitting in this minivan, but in a jail cell?"

D'neen's statement was on point and didn't warrant a response so Katrina offered none. D'neen closed her eyes thinking; one more day and all this will be over. She wondered what she would say to convince Ashley not to snitch to the police when they released her. Every idea or bribe D'neen thought of, she quickly dismissed as not being persuasive enough.

Ten minutes later, the minivan turned on to the dirt road that lead to the cabin and came to an abrupt stop. Katrina and D'neen were stunned to see a car coming to a stop in front of the cabin.

"Whose car is that?" Katrina asked.

"Like I'm supposed to know!"

"It could be Tasha."

"Someone's getting out --It's a man --He's waving to us? Do you think he's a cop?"

"I don't know!"

The man, who appeared to be in his fifties, walked toward the minivan. The first thing Katrina noticed about him was his stolid face.

"Pull off!"

"Relax! If he's a cop, they know where we live!"

"Shit, he's getting closer, pull off!"

"Relax bitch!"

D'neen wanted to yell back at Katrina, but the man was a foot away from the minivan walking up to Katrina's window.

"How y'all doing?"

Unable to speak, Katrina waved her hand, and D'neen nodded her head like a drone.

"Is that your place?"

Katrina hesitated, searching for a response, "It belongs to a friend."

The man looked back at the cabin as he said, "I remember this place was abandoned a few years back. I drove up here to see if it was still standing --Do you know if your friend is looking to sell?"

"No, they're going to fix it up?" Katrina said.

"Really?"

"Yes."

"I was hoping to buy it. Damn! Well here's my card, could you give it to your friend? Tell them to give me a call if they change their minds about selling."

"Okay," Katrina said taking the card.

"You ladies take care."

The man walked toward his car then stopped. He turned around and walked back to the minivan, Katrina and D'neen braced themselves believing that the guy was in fact going to reveal that he was the police and knew about Ashley inside.

"You think I can take a look inside?"

Katrina's heart kicked at her chest. D'neen placed her hand on the door knob ready to bolt from the minivan.

"I don't have a key, and the windows are boarded up."

The man chuckled shyly, "I understand, you girls probably want the place for yourselves --Well take it easy."

The man walked back to his car, got inside, then drove away honking his horn at Katrina and D'neen as he passed them.

"Do you believe him?" D'neen asked.

"Yeah. If he was the police, we'd be locked up now? Besides, his card says he's a realtor."

Katrina waited a moment then drove up to the cabin door. The women exited the minivan, D'neen carrying the McDonalds bag, Katrina lugging the knapsack. As they reached the door, Katrina stopped.

"I forgot the camcorder. D'neen could you get it from the back of the minivan?"

D'neen walked back to the minivan while Katrina entered the cabin. Katrina snickered at Ashley who looked indignant as she stood in front of the bed with her hands on her hips. With her back to Ashley, Katrina removed a stun gun from the knapsack, holding it behind her back as she walked casually up to Ashley. Before Ashley knew what had hit her, Katrina stunned her. Ashley fell on the bed screaming. Lucky for her, the volts in the gun were weak and caused little damage to her nervous system.

Hearing Ashley scream, D'neen raced into the cabin and caught a glimpse of the stun gun Katrina was dropping in the knapsack.

"What did you do?"

Katrina didn't respond, she walked over to the wooden table and sat down. In a look that resembled the cat that ate the canary, Katrina stared at D'neen with a mischievous grin. D'neen sat the McDonalds' bag on the table then rushed over to Ashley.

"Are you okay? What did she do?"

"That bitch is crazy, she tried to kill me! Why are you helping them? Get away from me!"

D'neen stood up looking guilty. Ashley moved against the wall, she sat up wrapping her arms around her legs. Ashley thought about the baby and prayed that everything was well.

"What all do you have in that knapsack?" D'neen asked.

"Don't question me."

"I'm not going to be a part of you hurting her."

"You already are."

Katrina's words hit home with D'neen. D'neen told herself, just one more day. She picked up the McDonalds' bag and dropped it on the bed next to Ashley.

"I know you don't expect me to eat that," Ashley said staring at the food with her stomach growling.

"Aren't you hungry?"

"I bet it's laced with poison."

"I wouldn't do that."

After Ashley shook off the effects of being stunned, she tore into the food. While eating she grumbled, "I don't usually eat McDonalds."

"How did you sleep Ashley?"

"Like a baby, I dreamed about Lewis."

Katrina started to respond but realized Ashley's only defense was to get under her skin.

"D'neen, empty Ashley's toilet under the bed."

"No!"

"Why not, your hands are already dirty. Tell her Ashley, she's just as guilty as me and Tasha," Katrina remarked as she picked up the pot and took it into the bathroom.

Ashley stood up peeking toward the bathroom, "D'neen you have to help me. Katrina's crazy and you know it. I think she even did something to my butt, it hurts."

D'neen wanted to say something, but her words were halted when Katrina entered the room. She walked between Ashley and D'neen and sat the pot next to the bed. D'neen walked over to the table, took a seat, then picked up the deck of cards on the table and began playing solitaire.

"Your piss stank. I can't believe my husband fucked your funky ass --D'neen, was you collaborating with the enemy? Tell me what she said to you. Did she ask you to free her?"

Before D'neen could respond, Ashley stood up asking, "Where is the other one?"

"What do you care?" Katrina asked, not looking for

an answer.

"You had your fun! Let me go," Ashley said in a softer tone. "Please Katrina, I promise I won't go to the police. You won't have anymore trouble out of me --I'll even move."

As Katrina walked across the room, she picked up the broken compact mirror from the floor, "I'm not superstitious, but you know what they say about broken mirrors Ashley."

"I'm not superstitious, so I don't care what they say."

"You should care, because it was bad luck to ever cross me," Katrina said in a sinister voice.

It was something in Katrina's voice that frightened D'neen causing her to stare at Katrina and wonder, how far was she willing to go. D'neen knew she had to do something crafty or things could end up badly for Ashley. Just as Katrina sat across from D'neen, Katrina's cell phone rang. She answered it.

"Hello, okay."

Katrina hung up the phone and motioned her head towards the door. D'neen got the cue and followed Katrina out the cabin.

"You have to go pick up Tasha."

"And leave you here alone with Ashley? Out of the question."

"What do you think, I'm going to let her go?"

D'neen responded to the sarcasm by rolling her eyes and turning her back to Katrina in an act of stubbornness.

"Okay, I'll be back in a half hour. D'neen, if you let her go, I'm going to shoot you and Charles and burn down y'all house with y'all dying inside."

D'neen listened in shock. Never before had her life been threatened, and hearing it left her speechless with her mouth agape.

"I have to get my knapsack," Katrina said, then darted in and out the cabin with knapsack in hand. D'neen was still in a bit of shock.

"D'neen, I was joking."

D'neen's fears subsided some as she watched Katrina hop in the minivan.

"D'neen, don't test me," Katrina warned in a stentorian voice before she drove off.

D'neen's mind was muddled as she walked back into the cabin and sat at the table visibly shaken. Ashley stood up looking generally concerned.

"D'neen, what happened?"

D'neen didn't speak. She was still trying to determine if Katrina was joking or serious.

"D'neen, I don't think you realize what you have gotten yourself into --This is selling drugs in front of a police station, y'all are going to prison."

"Shut up!" D'neen yelled standing abruptly.

"Calm down D'neen. I'm not your enemy. Katrina and Tasha are the ones who are manipulating you into doing something you don't want to do --You and I have no quarrel. I didn't sleep with Charles --"

"But you kissed him!"

"So you chain me like a dog? Conspire to kill me?"

"We're not going to kill you, we're letting you go tomorrow."

"You have to let me go now! That crazy bitch Katrina is not going to let me go! She can't risk it! And we don't know what Tasha will agree to."

"Why did you have to sleep with their husbands?"

"If you let me go, I won't go to the police. You can get tools, cut this lock off. You won't go to prison, I promise."

As D'neen listened, she believed Ashley wouldn't tell if she let her go. But could she cross Katrina, D'neen asked herself.

"D'neen, you're not like Katrina. Think about it, you have school coming up. Your whole life is ahead of you."

"Why did you sleep with their husbands and go after

Charles? You could have any man you want. I don't understand you, you have everything, and you're beautiful, famous, have a nice home and you drive around in a Bentley."

"You don't know shit! You don't know what I've been through. You wanna know why I sleep with so many men? It is because I hate them."

"How could you hate men when you give them your body freely then brag about it on the radio?"

"You ask too many questions, just let me the fuck go!"

"Why do you hate men?"

"Men are all dogs and opportunist --Now what? You wanna be a therapist? You are a fucking intern D'neen."

"Ashley, what happened to you?"

"I don't need to spill my heart out to you!"

Ashley's words belied her true feelings. She wanted badly to unload the secrets she had been carrying for too long. She exhaled ready to devolve her baggage.

"Ashley, you can talk to me," D'neen said pushing.

"D'neen, do you love your mother?"

"Of course."

"Would your mother give her life for you?"

"I believe she would."

"I bet your mother was the type that had breakfast on the table, talked with you about boys and sex and wiped your knees when you fell."

Ashley took a breather, she bit her bottom lip in anger turning to face the wall. She had D'neen's attention.

"When my stepfather first stuck it in me, I thought I was going to die --"

D'neen looked shocked as she walked over to the bed and sat next to Ashley.

"Yes, my mother let my stepfather molest me. Fuck molest, it was rape! My mother's advice was for me to stay away from him. It wasn't until I got pregnant that she actually acknowledged that the monster was raping me. And still, she did nothing."

"You didn't go to the police?"

"He threatened to kill me, and I believed him. Year after year, I endured him raping me. But it was all my fault according to my mother, because I was behaving too grown. His excuse was the drinking. You want to hear some scary shit? He used to choke me during the raping, and to cope with the pain, I made myself like it."

Ashley looked at D'neen for a reaction, but D'neen held her head down as her eyes were welled with tears.

Ashley chuckled, "I forced myself to like that shit, no wonder I'm screwed up now. I had no father, uncles, or brothers to protect me, so fuck men! I finally ran away and never went back. Now the bitch is sick and wants me to visit her. I would be there at this moment if I wasn't here chained like a dog. I don't care if she's sick, I was only going there to spit in her face. If I didn't leave there when I did, I would be in jail right now for double murder." Ashley yanked the cable, "D'neen, you have to let me go."

"I'm sorry about what happened to you. Tomorrow this will be over, I won't let Katrina or Tasha hurt you."

Ashley thought about revealing the possible cancer and the pregnancy, but decided she had told enough of her personal life.

"D'neen, I need you to let me go, please."

D'neen dropped her head contemplating doing the right thing and incurring the wrath of Katrina.

***

Karl entered his house a defeated man. It had been a few hours since he left Ashley's house and her closet-of-sex was still fresh in his mind. He had tried to call her, but to no avail. Now he was hoping that Sherri bought his story about finally seeing the light and telling Ashley that it was over between the two of them because his family meant more to him. Sherri entered the living room and saw Karl's forlorn face and went to him.

"Karl what's wrong?"

Karl didn't immediately respond. He had to play this one to the hilt because he knew Sherri could read him like a postcard. Karl looked at Sherri with puppy dog eyes.

"Baby, when I left here this morning, I won't lie, I left here ready to end it with us. But I drove around thinking about this family, my family, our family. I thought what was important…you and the children are what's important. So I told Ashley I never wanted to see her again."

Karl waited for a response as Sherri studied his eyes.

"Karl, if you don't want to be here, don't stay. Don't stay for no other reason but for your love for me and the kids."

"I love you and I told Ashley that."

As Karl and Sherri made up in bed, all he could think about was Ashley and what he had seen at her house.

***

Ashley cupped D'neen's face in her hands and stared intently in her eyes.

"Don't worry about them, do what you know is right."

D'neen stood up from the bed slowly. She walked over to the kitchen area and pondered her next move.

"Help me D'neen."

With what, D'neen searched the cabinets, "What am I doing, like it would be a lock cutter in here --I'm risking my life by helping you."

"If you don't help, I'm dead and you know it."

D'neen walked back over to the bed and examined the heavy duty lock.

"I'm going to need the key and Katrina has the only one."

"You can come back tonight with a lock cutter."

D'neen looked like she was losing her nerve as she thought about Ashley's suggestion. D'neen walked to the center of the room and stared at the floor in deep thought, nervously contemplating whether to cross Katrina.

"I don't know Ashley."

"Fuck Katrina, you let me go, and we go to the police together. Katrina will be arrested and after they find her guilty they'll throw the book at her and you will be safe."

"What about Tasha?"

"Fuck Tasha!"

D'neen walked over to the cable attachment bolted to wall. As she bent over checking the bolts to ascertain how tight they were, Katrina entered. D'neen stood slowly, Katrina glared at her.

"What were you doing?"

"Ashley was pulling on the cable like a wild woman and I was making sure the cable was secured."

"Really," Katrina said sarcastically.

"Where is Tasha?" D'neen asked.

Before Katrina could answer, Tasha entered carrying a small brown bag in one hand and a 7" portable DVD player in the other. D'neen walked over to Tasha and Katrina and pulled them in a huddle.

"Listen guys, it's a lot going on with Ashley that we didn't know about."

"Like what?" Tasha said in an unsympathetic voice.

"It's about her personal life."

"Fuck the whore's personal life," Tasha exclaimed.

"Are you trying to tell us that you fell for one of Ashley Gray's sob stories?"

"I have to use the bathroom," Ashley shouted.

"Why are you bothering us, use your potty," Katrina responded.

"Take this cable off my ankle so I can use the bathroom. I have to relieve myself!"

"D'neen, what were you saying?"

"Ashley had a reason for doing what she did to us, it isn't her fault."

"I have to use the bathroom!"

"Her screaming is annoying me, do something Katrina," Tasha said.

Katrina sighed, then walked over to the cable attachment on the wall. She checked the remaining length of the cable left in the apparatus and looked disappointed, "Shit, it's not enough cable for her to make it into the bathroom. Tasha I thought you checked it?"

"I did."

"D'neen and Tasha, come over here."

D'neen averted eye contact with Ashley as she walked over to Katrina. Tasha placed the DVD player on the table then walked over to the bed and dropped the brown bag on Ashley's lap. Tasha then joined Katrina and D'neen.

"Ashley, I'm going to unhook your ankle so you can use the bathroom. If you try something, I'm going to fuck you up."

"Hurry up!"

"Don't rush me, I might change my mind."

"You would love to see me shit in my drawers like a baby, wouldn't you?"

"I don't care."

"Please Katrina, unlock her so she can use the bathroom!" D'neen shouted.

Katrina dangled the key in front of Ashley's face several times teasingly. Each time Ashley reached for the key Katrina withdrew it. Frustrated with being toyed with, Ashley folded her arms across her chest until Katrina finally unlocked and removed the cable from around Ashley's ankle. Although Ashley was still a prisoner she felt a sense of freedom as she rubbed her ankle.

"You don't have time for that," Katrina said pointing towards the bathroom.

Ashley climbed off the bed glaring at the trio as she walked to the bathroom.

"Ashley's mother is very sick," D'neen whispered.

Katrina chuckled, "Oh, her dead mother is sick? And you believed that, didn't you? Ashley's mother died fifteen years ago, she told me that when we first met."

Katrina shook her head pitifully at D'neen who looked surprised and betrayed. Ashley exited the bathroom and looked at the cabin door. Katrina and Tasha stepped in front of her.

"Don't even think about it," Katrina said with her hands on her hips.

"Step aside, where am I going to run?"

The moment Katrina and Tasha moved an inch, Ashley saw the opportunity to escape. She pushed them both to the side and made a dash for the door. She would've made it if it wasn't for the fleet reaction of D'neen who tackled Ashley hard to the floor. Ashley grunted loudly. The crash to the floor wasn't the source of her pain, it was the fact that D'neen of all people prevented her escape.

"D'neen I'm going to get you!" Ashley yelled as she struggled on the floor with D'neen on top of her.

Katrina and Tasha joined the struggle. The trio managed to get a kicking and screaming Ashley back to the bed and locked the cable back around her ankle.

"I'm going to hurt you Ashley!" Katrina yelled.

"Fuck you!"

"D'neen you crossed me!"

"You lied! Your mother is not dead?"

"Tell her Ashley, your mother died fifteen years ago."

"As far as I'm concerned my mother is dead!"

Ashley sat on the bed frustrated, she clenched her fist and pounded the bed like a three year old throwing a tantrum. D'neen shook her head disappointedly then moped over to the table and sat down.

"That was fun," Katrina said breathing heavily.

"You hit me during the struggle," Tasha said rubbing her shoulder.

"You bitches are going to get it! Especially you D'neen, I can't wait…you dumb follower! I'm cold, hungry, my ass hurt, and I'm dirty! I need a bath! I demand a bath!" Ashley said looking disgusted.

"Act like a cat and lick yourself clean," Katrina offered.

"You do it for me," Ashley giggled, "You used to like that, didn't you? It would be like old times, right Katrina?"

"Imagine that."

Tasha and D'neen exchanged a surprised look. Tasha cut her eye at Katrina wondering if anything sexual had ever gone on between Ashley and Katrina.

"Tasha, you can get started," Katrina said.

Tasha walked over to the table, picked up the DVD player, and handed it to Katrina.

"D'neen, I need you to help me move the table over by the bed," Tasha said.

D'neen rose and helped Tasha carry the table a couple of feet away from the bed in front of Ashley. Katrina sat the DVD on the table and grabbed a chair. Tasha and D'neen also grabbed their chairs and placed them near the table. Tasha inserted a DVD in the player. On the screen was a home movie of Tasha and Bruce's wedding. The trio watched while Ashley at first turned away refusing to indulge. But the temptation was too much, she turned around to look.

"Ashley, do you see how happy we were?"

"Who cares, no one told you to marry a dog."

The next movie in the line of several, was the birth of Tasha's daughter, with Bruce sobbing as he videotape the delivery. Ashley thought about her own pregnancy and became emotional.

"You came in the middle of my family and ruined it," Tasha said choking with emotions.

With each home video of the daughter's birthday parties, anniversaries, and family events, Ashley's emotions grew as she began to understand how much she had hurt Tasha. After hours of watching videos and reliving the moments, Tasha broke down and cried loudly.

"I had enough. I can't take this. Let's go," Tasha said standing.

"We wanted you to see what you destroyed," Katrina said.

Ashley was too choked up to speak. The women gathered their things then left the cabin without saying a word. They climbed in the minivan with Katrina behind the wheel and headed home. Two minutes later, Ashley found her voice and uttered, "Tasha, I'm sorry."

Ashley sobbed, wallowing in her sadness for a total of five minutes. During that time, it was lost on her that she was the victim. She blamed herself for her predicament, but reality reemerged when she looked down at the cable attached to her ankle. Her anger returned, so did her hunger for freedom and food when she saw the brown bag Tasha had dropped on the bed. Ashley opened the bag and removed the bottled water and bologna sandwich which tasted like steak when she bit into it.

Once Ashley was finished with the sandwich, she began to plot her revenge against the girls in her head. Ashley thought about how she was going to get Tasha, but every sinister thought she had was smothered from the regret she felt while watching Tasha's home movies. In a decision that even surprised herself, Ashley abandoned her intentions on getting back at Tasha.

Next on Ashley's list was D'neen, who she considered a follower, and because of that Ashley would hire two thugs to beat D'neen to a pulp, guaranteeing a hospital stay. And for added measure, Charles would receive a beating as well for marrying the dumb bitch, Ashley concluded.

As for Katrina; Ashley rubbed her bald head thinking, then in a fit of rage, Ashley yelled, "You cut off my hair, I'll cut off your neck bitch!"

Ashley couldn't decide what she actually wanted to do to Katrina. However, she promised herself that whatever she did decide, it would be brutal enough to have a long lasting affect on her nemesis.

***

D'neen pulled into her driveway at 11:15 p.m. At that moment she remembered that her mother-in-law was scheduled to fly in earlier that day. D'neen cursed under her breath. After the day she had, she was in no mood to deal with her inquisitive mother-in-law. When D'neen exited her car and headed towards her house, she was so preoccupied with making up a story for her whereabouts, she didn't notice that Charles' car was not parked on the block.

D'neen entered her house quietly as she had done the night before. Since the house was dark, she assumed that Charles and his mother were probably asleep. D'neen crept upstairs. When she eased opened her bedroom door and didn't see Charles in bed, she assumed he was in the bathroom.

D'neen undressed quickly then climbed in bed. The coldness of the sheet was comforting upon her skin. She laid on her back then shifted to her side and closed her eyes pretending to be asleep. Ten minutes later when Charles hadn't come in the room, D'neen wondered what was keeping him.

She hopped out of the bed and walked to the bathroom, only to discover that it was empty. She moved down the hallway to the guest room and knocked on the door. When she didn't get an answer, she opened the door and found the room empty. She then walked slowly back to her bedroom and sat on the edge of the bed wondering where was Charles and his mother.

D'neen picked up her cell phone and called Charles. She was pissed when the call went to voice-mail. D'neen was too exhausted mentally to go into jealous wife mode, so she laid down on the bed and said, "One more day."

***

Unlike D'neen, Katrina and Tasha weren't ready to go home. They decided to spend a couple of hours at a crowded upscale bar. As they sat chatting, Katrina smiled at the handsome guy eyeing her from across the room. Tasha caught the exchange and looked annoyed. She thought about the statement Ashley had made about Katrina licking her body.

"What are you thinking about Tasha?"

"Nothing. Who are you smiling at?"

"Just a guy."

Tasha turned around eyeing the guy up and down, "He doesn't look all that."

"He's cute."

"And you're married."

"I know, but he's still cute isn't he? He's coming over here."

The sharply dressed handsome guy strolled over to Tasha and Katrina brandishing a smile and directing his words to Katrina.

"How y'all doing?"

"Okay," Katrina responded.

"Can I buy y'all a drink?"

"We're good," Tasha responded.

The guy gave Tasha a look as if to say, I wasn't talking to you. He then turned towards Katrina.

"What's your name?" Katrina asked.

"Joseph."

"Katrina, can I speak with you a moment?" Asked

Tasha, looking irritated.

The guy walked a couple feet away out of earshot, turning his back to the women as he nodded his head to the music.

"Let's get out of here and go back to my house. It's late, you can stay the night."

"We're having fun here."

"I'm ready to go Katrina."

"Don't go, we're enjoying ourselves. This is the first time I've been out in a long time."

"I'm tired, plus we have to discuss closing Ashley's situation. We can't hold her forever."

"We'll deal with that tomorrow. Tasha, you go home and get some rest. I'll call you in the morning."

"I don't want to leave you here alone."

"I'm cool, I know people here and I'm just going to stay for a half hour then go home."

"Okay…promise me that you won't go nowhere else but home."

"What?" Katrina asked chuckling.

"I'm serious, this guy don't look cool."

"What's up with you Tasha?"

"I'm just concerned about you."

"I'm a big girl."

"Just promise me that you won't drink too much."

"I promise. I'm just going to enjoy myself then go home."

"Go to your house from here, and watch your drink, don't let him slip nothing in it."

"I'm on it."

"Call me when you get home."

"Okay."

The girls embraced and mouthed goodbye. As Tasha walked past the guy she rolled her eyes. He winked his eye at her. She started to turn around and stay and play the third wheel, but she proceeded out the door.

"Was that your girlfriend?"

"Yeah."

"I didn't know," the guy said surprisingly.

Katrina realized what he was suggesting, "No, she's not my lady, she's a friend, my girl you know?"

"She looked jealous."

"No she didn't, you're tripping."

Thirty minutes later, Katrina danced out the bar on the arms of the handsome guy. He walked her to her car.

"You're going to follow me?" The guy asked.

"I'm going home, I told you I'm married."

"Come on baby, what he don't know can't hurt him."

The guy squeezed Katrina's butt causing a twitch between her legs. As her sexual arousal heightened, Katrina bit her bottom lip softly considering the adulterous invitation. She wanted badly to have sex, and even though her marriage was in the toilet, she was determined to hold to her convictions of being faithful even if Lewis wasn't.

"I have to go home," Katrina said nodding her head as if she was struggling with the decision, "Yeah, I have to get some rest. I have a big day tomorrow…I'm going to kill someone," Katrina said calmly.

The guy looked amused as he raised his eyebrow at Katrina waiting for her to smile or breakout laughing, revealing that she was joking. When she did neither, he felt she was either serious, or drunk. Whatever the case, it made no difference to the guy who was determined to get into Katrina's pants.

"When we leave my house tomorrow morning, I'll help you take out whoever you want to kill."

Katrina scoffed with a chuckle, reaffirming her belief that a man would say or do just about anything to get into a woman's pants.

"Okay, I'll follow you. How far do you live from here?"

"Ten minutes," the guy said cheerfully.

"Let's go baby, go get your car," Katrina said as she opened her car door.

The guy jogged to his car, hopped inside, then drove to the intersection and waited for Katrina. A few seconds later, Katrina drove up behind the guy and honked her car horn. The guy honked back then pulled off. At the next intersection the guy made a left. Katrina made a right and drove home laughing.

***

As Tasha parked her car at the curb in front of her house, she had no idea that she was being watched from the shadows. She sat behind the wheel regretting that she had left Katrina at the bar. She picked up her cell phone to call Katrina then paused thinking; how do I explain why I called?

So she removed the key from the ignition, exited the car and entered her house. As she attempted to close the door, a foot stepped into the doorway preventing the door from closing shut. Tasha froze in fear. She was about to scream, but didn't when she saw Bruce smiling with bloodshot eyes.

"Damn it, Bruce! You scared the shit out of me. Move your foot!"

"We have to talk."

Tasha fanned her hand in front of her face, "Oooh, I can smell your breath through the door. You're drunk," Tasha said as she kept pressure on the door, preventing Bruce from pushing it open.

"I know I'm drunk, but my mind is clear. I went to the hospital looking for you but you weren't there. I saw your boyfriend…how could you cheat on me with that pussy?"

"I didn't cheat on you and he's not my boyfriend. Now go back to where you're staying because I'm tired and want to go to sleep."

"Stop holding the door and let me in."

"No, leave!"

"I was wrong baby, and I'm sorry."

"I'm filled to the rim with your sorry ass."

"I'm sick of this shit!"

Bruce pushed opened the door causing Tasha to stumble back, but she didn't lose her footing. Bruce rushed to Tasha's aid holding her by the arms.

"I'm sorry baby."

"You could've hurt me Bruce."

"I'm sorry, just hear me out."

"No!"

"Please."

"You got two minutes."

"Okay, I want to say again I'm sorry. That bitch tricked me --I was at the light minding my own business--"

Tasha looked annoyed as she sighed, "I don't want to hear this."

"She tricked me," Bruce raised his index finger seemingly checking himself, "Yeah, you don't want to hear about that. I want to be with my family, you and my daughter."

Tasha glanced at her watch, "Okay, your two minutes are up, we'll talk tomorrow."

Bruce ignored Tasha and headed for the stairs. Tasha rushed over to him and arrested his arm stopping him from mounting the stairs.

"Where do you think you're going?"

"I'm going to see my daughter."

"She isn't here, she's at your sister's house."

"That's right."

"Okay, let's go."

Tasha turned Bruce around guiding him by the arm to the door. She thought he was leaving peacefully until he stopped a couple feet away from the door.

"No, I'm not leaving!"

"Yes you are," Tasha said giving him a shove.

"No, this is my house too. I told my mother that I was coming back to my house!"

"Your house! How many times are we going to go through this? This is my house, in my name. I pay the bills. When was the last time you had a job and helped with a bill? All you did here was eat, sleep, fuck me, and call out another woman's name when you had your nasty ass dick in my mouth! Did you tell your mother that?" Tasha said with emphasis as she waggled her face in Bruce's.

Bruce was hurt as he listened to Tasha stampede upon his manhood. As she continued to berate and ridicule him, Tasha didn't notice the change in Bruce's bloodshot eyes. They moved from embarrassment to anger.

Bruce's mind, already befuddled with alcohol, became violent. In a sudden rage, he seized Tasha by her arms backing her to the sofa. He threw Tasha down on the sofa and hopped on top of her, pressing her down with the weight of his body. Tasha screamed profanities and twisted violently underneath Bruce's body.

"You want me to scream your name, I will!"

"Get the hell off me Bruce!"

"You think you can keep disrespecting me."

"You're hurting me!"

"I'm your husband."

Bruce maneuvered Tasha's arms above her head. With a strong hand, he held her wrist together.

"Bruce, you're hurting my wrist!"

Bruce laid his mouth upon Tasha's to muffle her screams. As Bruce sexually assaulted his wife, he moaned out her name repeatedly. Hearing her own name being moaned was sickening to Tasha's ears. She wished she could make him shut up, but she was powerless, Bruce was too strong and determined.

Tasha thought the assault would never end. She felt like a stranger was violating her insides. In an act to hasten the ordeal, she pumped back in rhythm with Bruce. It worked. Seconds later Bruce relieved himself and collapsed on Tasha's sweaty body. One angry tear fell from her eye.

"Are you happy now, I called your name."

Tasha felt humiliated. She slapped Bruce hard against his face then pushed him. As Bruce was falling to the floor, the back of his hand accidentally caught Tasha hard under her eye.

"Aaaah! You slapped me!"

"It was an accident, I was falling. Why did you push me on the floor?" Bruce said sitting against the sofa.

Tasha stood up, glared at Bruce, then hurried upstairs to the bathroom. She stood in the shower scrubbing her vagina vigorously. This was the first time she ever felt dirty in her life. She now knew how the many rape victims felt when they walked into the hospital whispering to a doctor or nurse that they had been raped.

After Tasha finished showering, she looked at her reflection in the mirror. She stared at the swelling underneath her eye. She cursed and grimaced, figuring the eye would be black in the morning.

Tasha walked downstairs and saw Bruce asleep on the sofa. Bruce was so tired when he had climbed on the sofa from his fall to the floor, he didn't bother to pull up his pants that were still down to his ankles. As Tasha frowned at him, she thought, you dirty dog.

Tasha walked into the kitchen and removed a tray of ice from the freezer. As she placed the ice in a towel, she recalled something Katrina had said she had done to Lewis. Tasha sat the ice on the table then grabbed a butcher's knife and crept back into the living room and stood over Bruce.

With a wicked grin on her face, Tasha kneeled down and began stroking Bruce's penis. He awoke groggily and smiled at Tasha, but his smile was washed away when he saw the sparkle from the blade of the butcher knife as Tasha raised it. Bruce jumped back, kicking Tasha along the way. The kick was more of a reaction than intentional.

Tasha fell back hitting her head against the coffee table. Bruce jumped to his feet and placed his hand over his mouth when he saw Tasha not moving. He kneeled down and lifted her head off the floor.

"Tasha, Tasha, Tasha," Bruce mumbled as he began to sob.

When Tasha didn't respond, he patted her cheek and looked around, lost as to what to do. When he gained his senses he called 911, telling the police an accident had taken place. He didn't give the police his name, but he gave Tasha's address then hung up. He lifted Tasha's limped body and laid her gently on the sofa.

Bruce sat on the sofa, resting Tasha's head on his lap. He was grateful when he checked and found a pulse. As he begged Tasha to wake up, he noticed the swelling underneath her eye. His mind began to think the worst; if the cops saw Tasha's eye, they would believe that he had battered her since he had a criminal record.

Bruce felt that he couldn't take a chance of being arrested. He believed it would be best for the police to take Tasha to the hospital without asking him a thousand questions.

Reluctantly, Bruce stood up. He shook his head at Tasha, leaned down and kissed her on the forehead, then hurried out the house leaving the door ajar.

Five minutes later, from down the block, Bruce watched the paramedic carry Tasha's body on a gurney into the ambulance then drive away. Bruce called Tasha's sister and told her what had happened.

CHAPTER 35

D'neen awoke at 6:00 a.m. tired as if she hadn't slept at all. The stress of the kidnapping was taking a toll on her. For a moment, she stared at Charles laying sound asleep next to her and snoring moderately. She wanted to awake him and seek his advice about the kidnapping, but on the other hand, she didn't want him involved, for his own protection against any possible future prosecution.

D'neen had been asleep when Charles crept in at 4:35 a.m. from a night of clubbing, something he wasn't accustomed to doing.

D'neen climbed quietly out of bed, put on her robe, then walked down the hall to the guest room. After a couple of soft knocks and no answer, D'neen cracked opened the door and peeked inside. She was happy to see the room empty of her mother-in-law.

D'neen made her way into the kitchen. She removed a box of Captain Crunch cereal from the cabinet and poured a bowl full and added milk. As she watched the cereal float in the bowl, she thought about the day ahead; she was to meet Katrina and Tasha at the minivan at 7 o'clock. She glanced at the clock, it was a quarter to six. Each woman had to offer their suggestions on the best bribe to persuade Ashley not to snitch when they released her.

D'neen's suggestion would be for each woman to pool their money and offer Ashley a payoff. D'neen knew Katrina and Tasha would reject the suggestion because it was her fault that Ashley discovered their identities, but this was all she could come up with. D'neen hoped that Tasha's home video had an effect on Ashley, giving her a sense of why she was kidnapped. And maybe then she wouldn't be so hell-bent on going to the police.

D'neen placed her bowl in the sink then headed back to her bedroom. Charles was still asleep. In the instant that she wondered what time he had come home, D'neen's mind wandered into suspicious mode.

She picked up his pants and searched his pockets like a common thief. As she sat his pants back down, she looked over at Charles and was startled to see him staring back at her with disappointed eyes. D'neen smiled, attempting to hide her embarrassment.

"What were you looking for?"

With her hand caught in the cookie jar, D'neen used a frequently used tactic in this kind of situation, she turned the tables on Charles putting him of the defensive.

"What time did you get home?"

"You haven't answered my question. What were you looking for?"

"Where were you all night, I went to sleep at one and you wasn't here."

"What were you looking for in my pockets?"

D'neen used the second most used tactic, she walked out the room in the middle of the argument.

"D'neen!" Charles yelled.

D'neen heard Charles calling her but ignored him. She suspected that his next question would be about her whereabouts for the past two days. She shot in the bathroom and took a shower, taking the time to come up with a story. As she let the hot water from the shower dance on her face, she couldn't wait to get to the cabin and let Ashley go so she could concentrate on her marriage and get things back as they were before.

After the shower, D'neen walked back into the

bedroom. Charles was sitting upright and waiting for her.

"When did you start ignoring me?"

"I didn't hear you, I was in the bathroom."

"Really," Charles said chuckling.

"I don't want to argue. I was looking through your pocket for what, I don't know. That's how women are, spontaneous, nosy, and very jealous. Now I don't want to talk about this no more."

Charles was taken aback by D'neen's assertiveness. He remained silent as he watched her dress. He knew when he asked where she was going, she would respond, "With the girls." Charles fought the feeling, but he was beginning to suspect that D'neen was cheating.

"Where are you going?"

"I told you, me and the girls are going shopping --"

"This fucking early?"

"Why are you cursing at me?"

"Are you really going shopping and hanging out with these so-called girls of yours?" Charles said sarcastically.

"You can ask Katrina --"

"Fuck Katrina, I don't know her!"

D'neen knew her marriage was taking a turn for the worse, so she sat on the bed, pulled Charles close to her, and told him an elaborate lie.

***

Across the street, Katrina had awakened at 6:00 a.m. She only managed to get two hours of sleep because of the heated argument she had with Lewis when she came home from the bar. When she walked through the door, Lewis stood waiting in the living room with a barrage of questions and accusations. There was shouting, cursing, and name calling that lead to pushing and shoving, but nothing violent.

For the most part, the physical part of the fight was initiated by Katrina. All Lewis did was defend himself by holding Katrina by her arms tightly preventing her from hitting him.

The fighting came to halt when Katrina said that she should've went home with the handsome guy from the bar. It took every bit of restraint in Lewis not to knock Katrina out with a punch to her sassy mouth.

Katrina climbed out of bed and headed into the bathroom. As she showered, she thought about the day ahead; she didn't think about a bribe for Ashley. Katrina knew what she wanted and intended on doing, but her problem was how to get away with it.

Katrina dressed quickly, then glanced at her watch. It was 6:47, she was running late. She walked down into the basement to get her gun but was surprised to see Lewis lifting weights in front of the place where she had hid the gun, she cursed under her breath.

"What are you doing down here?" Lewis asked.

"How long are you going to be working out?"

"Why?"

"I just want to know, are you training for me?" Katrina said tauntingly.

Lewis didn't answer, he continued with his lifting. Katrina wanted to get the gun and shoot Lewis in the leg, but she nixed the idea believing that he was such a pussy that he would tell on her. When it looked like Lewis would be awhile, she abandoned the gun and walked upstairs, grabbed her car keys, then left the house.

CHAPTER 36

Karl was the first to awake in his household. This was typical for Sunday morning. He laid still in bed, staring at the ceiling wondering what Ashley was doing at this precise moment. He tried to shake the thought of her, but she lingered in his mind refusing to go away. He wondered, was she at her mother's house, or laying on the chest of another man while they slept, or perhaps she could be laying alone in her own bed thinking of him.

Karl knew he shouldn't concern himself with Ashley and her affairs. He had made the decision to reconcile with Sherri and this time he was determined to remain faithful to her both physically and mentally. He looked to his left and watched her sleeping peacefully. He noted how beautiful she was and felt grateful that the mother of his children was faithful and forgiving.

Karl decided to surprise the family by making them breakfast. He climbed out of bed silently and went to the kitchen. As he passed the telephone, he had the sudden urge to call Ashley, but he fought the desire.

Karl opened the refrigerator scanning the contents searching for something easy to cook. When he made his decision, he scrambled eggs, fried the sausages, and then toasted the bread. After setting the plates, he was about to call the family down to eat when the urge to call Ashley resurfaced, this time he couldn't fight it. He picked up the phone, dialed Ashley, and was disappointed to get her voice-mail.

Sherri awakened to the aroma of the food cooking in the kitchen. She smiled warmly knowing that Karl was attempting to do something he hadn't done before, cook a meal for the family. She hoped the food was good and if it wasn't, she would eat it anyway, and with pleasure because her loving husband had cooked it.

She hurried down the stairs toward the kitchen then slowed her pace deciding to sneak up on Karl, hoping to catch him in front of the stove wearing an apron around his waist. As she stepped silently into the kitchen entrance, she stopped.

Karl's back was to Sherri, he was on the phone and not aware of her presence. He had decided to call Ashley back and leave a message. It would be a decision he would come to regret. Sherri boiled with anger as she listened to Karl speak into the phone, stating that he and Ashley needed to talk and that he cared deeply for her.

Sherri had heard enough. She backed out of the kitchen with her stomach in knots and eyes welled with tears. She plodded up the stairs and entered her bedroom locking the door. She curled up on the bed and sobbed. Five minutes later, Karl yelled upstairs for the family to come down for breakfast.

As the family sat at the table eating, Karl was so busy joking with the children that he didn't notice that Sherri was distant.

After breakfast, Karl told Sherri that he had to go out for an hour and when he returned home, she and the children are to be dressed and ready for an afternoon family outing. Karl kissed Sherri on her cheek then hurried out the door. Five minutes after Karl left, Sherri left out the house as well. Her intuition told her where he was headed.

Karl pulled his car to the curb in front of Ashley's house. He hopped out, jogged to the house, then knocked on the door. A few seconds later, he rang the bell. When Ashley didn't answer, he used his key and entered the house. He yelled out Ashley's name several times before walking upstairs to her bedroom. He observed that the room was undisturbed from the day before, so he left out the house.

As he walked toward his car, he saw the sedan driving slowly up the block. The car looked familiar, but he paid it no mind. As he walked around the front of his car and headed for the driver's side door, the sedan, which by now was ten yards away, burst into speed. Before Karl had time to react, the sedan plowed into him, causing him to fly several feet backwards landing on his back.

Karl screamed in pain. Sherri hopped out the sedan and raced over to him yelling.

"Motherfucking liar! You got a key to that bitch's house! I'll fucking kill you!"

As Karl groaned in pain, Sherri continued cursing, oblivious to the fact that he was seriously injured. Lewis was the first neighbor to exit his house when he heard Sherri screaming at her wounded husband on the ground for cheating. Lewis glanced at Ashley's house, then back to the commotion, and knew Ashley had struck again.

CHAPTER 37

At 7:30 a.m. Sunday, Ashley awoke with an attitude. She sat upright, then stretched her arms over her head and yawned as she looked around the cabin, thankful that this was her last day here. That was if D'neen had spoken the truth about letting her go on Sunday.

Ashley had no sense of the time, but since she was an early riser, she figured it was before 8 o'clock. As her stomach growled, she wondered where the Three Stooges were. With each minute that passed, Ashley's anxiety grew. So she stood up and began to jog in place like she was on a treadmill, seemingly to reduce her built up stress.

After five minutes of exercise on an empty stomach, she tired out and sat on the edge of the bed. She smelled her armpit, squinting her nose from the odor of not washing in three days. Of all the things Ashley wanted to attain in life, they all seemed trivial at the moment compared to the hot bath she desired and needed.

Ashley felt the urge to pee and sighed. Once again she had to subject herself to some backwoods shit, as she put it. She pulled the pot from underneath the bed then squatted and peed. Not being able to properly clean herself added to the distress she felt during the whole ordeal of her kidnapping.

Ashley sat back on the bed and stretched her neck from side to side trying to stay optimistic, but it was tough. She thought, for a fellow woman to subject her to not being able to bathe, eat properly, and wipe herself when she peed was deplorable. “Oooooooh, I’m going to get these bitches,” Ashley uttered as she punched her right fist into her left palm.

As Ashley killed the time thinking of a way to pay back Katrina, an unwelcoming thought kept entering her mind. The thought of Katrina not letting her go began to trouble her. Ashley tried to dismiss the thought as unimaginable, but the possibility of the thought remained.

Ashley knew she had to do something to protect herself against Katrina should the time come that Katrina wanted to get seriously violent. Ashley looked around the cabin for a weapon, but her search was fruitless. The only thing tangible in the cabin was the wooden table, chairs, and the pot with piss in it.

The moment she was about to give up hope finding a weapon, she saw a piece of the broken mirror on the floor. Ashley jumped off the bed, laid on the floor, and outstretched her arms and fingers, but the mirror was still several feet out of reach. She cursed in frustration.

Ashley had an idea. She rushed over to the bed, removed the sheet and tied the end into a knot. She laid back on the floor, and on her first try, she slung the sheet over the broken mirror and pulled it to her.

As she sat on the edge of the bed staring at the three inch piece of mirror in her hand, she felt empowered and dangerous. She hid her weapon under the pillow, then waited.

CHAPTER 38

Katrina was the first to arrive on the block where she, Tasha, and D'neen rendezvoused before driving up to the cabin in the minivan. Katrina parked her car, removed the black knapsack from the trunk, then climbed behind the wheel of the minivan. She glanced at her watch, it was 7:20 a.m. She wondered why everyone was late. For a second, she toyed with the idea of driving up to the cabin alone for a one on one with Ashley.

"Damn!" Katrina said out of the blue.

She smacked the steering wheel with her palm remembering that she was supposed to call Tasha last night when she got home from the bar. She hoped Tasha wouldn't be so whiny about the matter when she saw her.

Katrina picked up the camcorder and played back the footage of Ashley on the first night at the cabin. As Katrina viewed the footage on the small screen, her eyes were wide with delight as she watched the fear in Ashley's eyes, not to mention her bald head. Katrina turned off the camcorder, leaned her head back against the head-rest, and closed her eyes.

She began to go over the day's plan in her head; she would of course fuck with Ashley as much as Tasha and D'neen allowed. When the time came, she would inject Ashley with Chloral Hydrate, sedating her. Ashley would be taken to her car to awake about an hour later free to do as she pleased. But lurking nearby, out of sight will be Katrina with gun in hand ready to shoot Ashley and be done with the matter. Katrina looked at it as payment for her loss, which she attributed to Ashley.

As Katrina continued to wallow in her thoughts, D'neen drove up, parked her car, then opened the passenger's side door, startling Katrina.

"What are you doing sneaking up on me?"

"And good morning to you too."

"You're late."

"Where's Tasha?"

"She's late too."

"I have my suggestion on how we are going to let Ashley go."

"Call Tasha, we're running late."

D'neen called Tasha but got her voice-mail.

"No answer. Do you think she went to work?"

"No, she would've called me first."

"Here's my suggestion…"

Katrina barely listened as D'neen related her suggestion to bribe Ashley.

"Call Tasha again," Katrina said cutting off D'neen.

Once again D'neen called Tasha and got her voice-mail.

"No answer."

Katrina started the minivan and pulled off.

"Where are you going?"

"Tasha's place."

"What if she comes here and we're not here?"

"She'll call me."

When Katrina arrived on Tasha's block, the first thing she noticed was Tasha's car parked in front of her door. Katrina doubled parked, hopped out the minivan, then rang Tasha's doorbell and knocked on the door several times without getting an answer. As Katrina contemplated what to do next, a neighbor exited her house and walked over to Katrina.

"Are you looking for Tasha?"

"Yes."

"The police was here last night --"

"What?" Katrina said loud enough for D'neen to hear and looked over.

"They took Tasha away in an ambulance."

"What happened?"

"I don't know. Someone said she walked in on a burglar, but nobody really knows what happened but Tasha?"

"Do you know what hospital she was taken to?"

"Jefferson."

"Good, that's where she works --Thank you."

"I haven't seen her husband around in weeks, I think there was trouble between them --Do you know any of her family's numbers?"

"No, I wish I did."

"Thank you," Katrina said. She hopped in the minivan and sped off. As Katrina headed for the hospital, she made a mental note to herself to get Tasha's family's information for future reference.

"What's going on?"

"Tasha is in the hospital."

"What happened?"

"Nobody knows."

Katrina arrived in the hospital parking lot in record time. She and D'neen raced into the hospital. D'neen nearly bumped into a man in a neck brace laying on a gurney and being rushed down the hall, with a woman trailing along side screaming at the man for cheating on her. D'neen held her hand over her mouth shocked to see that the man was Karl.

"That's Ashley's boyfriend, the woman must be his wife. She was saying that he shouldn't have cheated on her," D'neen said pulling on Katrina's arm and pointing at Karl being moved down the corridor.

"I told you we were doing the right thing."

After getting Tasha's room number, Katrina and D'neen walked briskly down the corridor. Up ahead they witnessed the police putting handcuffs on Sherri and leading her out the hospital. When Katrina and D'neen reached Tasha's room, they hesitated a moment as they exchanged concerned looks, then entered the room.

Tasha was in the bed with a bandage around her head, her sister was standing at her bedside. When Tasha saw her friends her face lit up.

"Katrina, D'neen."

Katrina and D'neen walked over to the bed and looked at Tasha with sad eyes.

"How are you doing?" D'neen asked.

"Hey Tasha," said Katrina staring at Tasha's black eyes.

"I'm going to be okay. Katrina, D'neen, this is my sister Lynn."

The women exchanged their greetings.

"I'm going to get some coffee. Do anyone need a cup."

Both D'neen and Katrina shook there heads no.

"I'll be back in a couple of minutes."

Lynn left the room. Katrina and D'neen moved closer to Tasha's bedside.

"What happened?" Katrina asked.

"Bruce --"

"Bruce!" Katrina and D'neen yelled simultaneously.

"It wasn't like y'all think."

"He punched you," Katrina said.

"It was an accident."

"But you have a black eye and you're in the hospital," D'neen said pointing out the obvious.

"This is what happened. After I left you, I went home, opened my door, and entered my house. As I tried to close the door, Bruce's drunken ass stuck his foot in the doorway --to make a long story short, Bruce raped me, then accidentally kicked me. I fell back and hit my head…I had a concussion and some bleeding --"

"That motherfucker," said Katrina.

"Is he locked up?"

"No --I didn't tell the police."

"Why?"

"He's my daughter's father. Besides, it was an accident."

"Was the rape an accident?" Katrina asked.

Tasha didn't have an answer. It was a moment of silence until Katrina spoke.

"Fuck the police, we can get him ourselves!"

Tasha chuckled, "Forget it, I'm divorcing him and moving on."

"He needs to pay," Katrina insisted.

"We already got one person locked away," Tasha responded.

"We're letting her go today right?" D'neen said, hoping Tasha and Katrina would confirm her statement.

Katrina didn't respond.

"Katrina y'all have to let Ashley go. Do what y'all must to convince her not to snitch."

"I'll take care of it," Katrina said smiling at D'neen.

"Well, y'all go do what y'all have to do…make it happen."

"Tasha, give your sister my phone number."

"Okay."

D'neen hugged Tasha and said goodbye. Katrina followed up with a hug as well.

"I'm sorry Tash," Katrina said.

"What for?"

"I should've left with you last night."

"This isn't your fault, Bruce and his drinking."

"Don't worry, he's going to get what he's got

coming, I promise."

"Just take care of that business with Ashley."

Lynn entered the room, "Whose Ashley?"

D'neen looked nervous. Katrina smiled thinking Lynn could take Tasha's place.

"Nobody. Lynn give me a pencil and paper so I can give you Katrina and D'neen's number."

After the women exchanged their goodbyes, Katrina and D'neen left. As Katrina drove to the cabin, all she could think of was getting Bruce. After all, she blamed herself for Tasha's situation. Katrina turned the minivan onto the road that led to the cabin. Little did she and D'neen know, Tasha had slipped into a coma ten minutes after they left her?

CHAPTER 39

Lewis sat on the weight bench in his basement exhausted and breathing heavily from an hour and forty minutes of an intense weight and cardiovascular workout. As he sat there recuperating, a thought crossed his mind causing him to rub his chin curiously about something Katrina had done. Lewis stood slowly looking around the basement, wondering why Katrina had come down into the basement earlier.

Lewis found that act particularly odd because Katrina never came in the basement for anything. Maybe she had come down to see what he was doing, Lewis thought, then rejected that notion because Katrina didn't care what he did around the house. He concluded that Katrina had come into the basement for a specific reason but his presence deterred her from whatever she was planning to do or retrieve.

Lewis recalled that Katrina had been acting strangely the last couple days. He had assumed that she was cheating, but now he believed it could be something more.

Lewis began to casually check the basement looking for something out of the ordinary. His heart rate increased when he found a two inch, plain box behind two large cardboard boxes. But he was disappointed when he opened the small box and found it empty.

After ten minutes of searching and coming up with nothing but dust, Lewis found Katrina's 38 revolver. He held the cold steel in his hand. He stared at the firearm as if it was a foreign object. This wasn't the first gun Lewis held in his hands, but it was the first gun he held that belonged to his temperamental wife.

As Lewis studied the gun, the question of why Katrina had a gun hit him like a baseball bat against his kneecaps. It was to kill, he assumed. The thought of being murdered shook him. His legs became weak, so he sat on the weight bench. He was thankful Katrina hadn't discovered that he had resumed his relationship with Ashley. If Katrina had, he probably would be dead, he reckoned. He was even more thankful that Ashley had kicked him to the curb.

Lewis thought about how Katrina had put the knife to his neck and threatened him. He concluded that it was really time for a divorce, he wondered how he was going to handle this situation with the gun. The silly part of his brain suggested that he put the gun back, from there he would just keep an eye on Katrina to see what she was up to. But the sensible part of his brain overrode the nonsense he had just thought causing him to almost scream out loud, are you crazy?

He took the bullets out of the gun, put them in his pocket, then walked up the stairs with the gun in hand and waited for Katrina to return.

CHAPTER 40

Katrina and D'neen sat in the parked minivan in front of the cabin. Katrina looked distant as she stared blankly through the windshield out into the woods thinking about Tasha. She thought about how Tasha had described the beating Vern received at the hands of Bruce at the hospital. The thought of Tasha receiving that same treatment made Katrina clench her teeth in anger.

"What are you thinking about?" D'neen asked.

"Nothing."

D'neen knew what Katrina was thinking about because she herself was thinking about Tasha also.

"It's a shame what Bruce did, he should be in jail…Are you ready to go inside…We agreed that we were letting Ashley go. I'll offer her the money…then you can open the lock," D'neen said, hoping to get a favorable response from Katrina.

"What if she doesn't take the bribe?" Katrina said cynically.

"She'll take it."

"What if she doesn't D'neen?"

"She will, I know she will."

"You hope she will. D'neen, I'm not going to jail."

D'neen didn't respond. She couldn't conceive Ashley not taking the bribe or the kidnapping going on longer than today. Katrina grabbed the knapsack from the back seat.

"Katrina, whatever you're thinking about doing to

Ashley, forget it, we're letting her go. Tormenting her will just make matters worse."

Katrina ignored D'neen and got out of the minivan. D'neen sighed, then followed Katrina.

"D'neen, I left something in the minivan, could you get it for me?"

D'neen stopped for a second. She was about to go back to the minivan, but she caught herself realizing that Katrina was trying to trick her again.

"I'm not falling for that again."

"Just give me five minutes alone with Ashley then we'll let her go."

The offer was tempting, but D'neen couldn't risk it, so she shook her head no. When Katrina and D'neen entered the cabin, Ashley was sitting on the edge of the bed with her arms folded across her chest. The first thing Ashley noticed was that neither woman had food, which she viewed as a good sign because there was no need for food if they were letting her go.

The second thing Ashley noticed was the infamous black knapsack Katrina was holding, which meant Katrina was still up to no good.

"Okay y'all had your fun, now let me out of this thing."

"Are you going to the police?" Katrina asked

"No, I'll let bygones be bygones," Ashley said sincerely.

D'neen looked happy as she nodded to Katrina, who didn't share her enthusiasm.

"Do you believe her D'neen," Katrina said as she sat at the table looking inside the knapsack.

"Ashley, we are willing to give you five thousand dollars," D'neen said.

"I spend that kind of money shopping on the weekends."

"Plus, we'll give you money every week for six

months."

Katrina picked up the wooden chair, walked over in front of Ashley, and sat before her, lighting a cigarette.

"My friend is in the hospital because of you," Katrina said as she stood up and flicked ashes on Ashley.

"Bitch watch it!" Ashley shouted.

"Katrina, stop it!"

Katrina laughed, then sat back in her chair and finished her cigarette. As Ashley and Katrina stared at each other in silence, Ashley was beginning to believe that Katrina's hatred for her ran deeper than the affair with Lewis, but Ashley couldn't put her finger on what it was.

"Are you going to take the money?" D'neen asked.

"Well, I don't know."

Katrina plucked the cigarette at Ashley. It would have landed on Ashley's lap if she didn't scoot back. Ashley flailed the cigarette off the bed. Before she could curse Katrina as she intended to do, D'neen stood in front of Katrina.

"You are trying to screw this up!"

"Tasha is in the hospital and you defend this bitch!"

"It's time to let her go!"

"Fuck her!'

Ashley stood abruptly, "Fuck you Katrina! Let me go now before I change my mind about going to the police."

Katrina stepped to Ashley and slapped her hard across the face, then walked over to the table and picked up the knapsack. Ashley didn't respond. She sat on the bed looking angry without speaking. D'neen looked upset as she whispered to Katrina.

"You're acting like you don't want to let her go. Just give me the key so we can get the fuck out of here?"

"I left the key home."

D'neen looked bewildered as she said nothing. Katrina removed a can of lighter fluid from her knapsack and hid it behind her back as she walked to Ashley in a creeping mode.

"What do you have behind your back?" D'neen demanded to know.

Without warning, Katrina squirted lighter fluid on Ashley.

"What the hell is this!" Ashley said as she smelled the lighter fluid and frantically tried to wipe it off with the sheet.

"You are out of your mind," D'neen said in disbelief as she helped Ashley wipe off the fluid.

"You are sick!" Ashley shouted.

Katrina lit a cigarette and walked closer towards Ashley and D'neen.

"Katrina no!" D'neen yelled as she moved away from Ashley.

Katrina plucked the cigarette at Ashley who jumped out the way of the cigarette.

"Stop it, you're going to burn her!"

Katrina squirted more lighter fluid on Ashley as she went hysterical. D'neen grabbed Katrina's arm. Katrina pulled away and lit another cigarette. This time she smoked the cigarette and stared at Ashley who glared back at Katrina as she dried herself.

"D'neen, you're going to jail if you don't stop her!"

"Katrina, please, this has to end."

Ashley remembered the mirror under the pillow. The first opportunity she got she was going to reach for it and inflict as much harm on Katrina as possible. Katrina walked over to Ashley and shoved her. Ashley was so pissed, she stood abruptly in front of Katrina defiantly. But Katrina was unmoved, she pushed Ashley to the bed. Again Ashley stood, this time she grabbed hold of Katrina and wrestled her to the bed. Ashley reached under the pillow and grabbed the mirror.

Ashley tried to slice Katrina across the forearm, but Katrina grabbed Ashley's wrist then head-butted her causing her to give up the fight as she was dazed. Katrina took the mirror out of Ashley's hand and wedged it against Ashley's neck.

"I should cut your damn throat."

"Don't do it Katrina, please don't do it," D'neen begged.

Katrina made a light slice causing a little blood. Ashley grunted in pain. Katrina threw the broken mirror then slapped a sobbing Ashley across the face.

"Stop hitting me, I'm pregnant!"

Katrina and D'neen both looked surprised. Katrina stood up and looked down at Ashley.

"You'll say anything to keep me off your ass."

"I am pregnant."

"I don't give a fuck," Katrina said giving Ashley a light push as Ashley sat up.

"Katrina, she said she's pregnant. You can't put your hand on a pregnant woman."

"That only applies to men."

"Lewis could be the father."

Katrina's face was distorted with anger. Ashley realized she made a mistake.

"Katrina, it was Lewis, he wouldn't leave me alone."

"You're a fucking liar."

"Where is Lewis now huh? I'll tell you where. He's in Miami, he wanted me to go with him but I refused."

Katrina knew Lewis was supposed to go to Miami, but he cancelled it because he wasn't sure what Katrina was up to.

"You are not pregnant."

"I can prove it. I have a prescription for prenatal vitamins in my pocketbook. Where is my pocketbook?"

Katrina stared silently at Ashley for a moment, then grabbed the knapsack and stormed out the cabin. D'neen ran behind her, not before telling Ashley that she would be back.

"Where are you going Katrina?"

Katrina didn't respond as she hopped behind the wheel of the minivan. D'neen looked confused, then hopped in the passenger's seat and put on her seatbelt as Katrina sped off. Twenty minutes later the minivan came to a stop in front of the parking lot where D'neen had parked Ashley's car.

Katrina jogged over to Ashley's car, opened the door, grabbed Ashley's pocketbook from underneath the seat, and searched it and found the prescription. As Katrina read the prescription, D'neen walked up behind Katrina and read the prescription for herself.

"She's pregnant," Katrina said in a broken voice.

"So, it doesn't mean that Lewis is the father."

Katrina tossed the pocketbook back underneath the seat, closed the door then walked slowly towards the minivan in a daze. She and D'neen got in the minivan. Katrina didn't start the ignition as she just sat there staring glassy eyed out the window. It was like the life had been drained out of her.

"Let's just go back to the cabin and let her go and whatever happens, happens."

Katrina didn't respond. Her eyes were welled with tears as the pain in her stomach grew. Katrina was so out of it that the ringing of her cell phone startled her. She answered in a weak voice, "Hello?"

Katrina listened as Tasha's sister Lynn revealed that Tasha had died.

"Nooo!" Katrina said with tears streaming down her cheeks.

She dropped the phone in her lap and pounded the stirring wheel with her palm. D'neen picked up the phone and asked, "Who is this…Lynn, this is D'neen. Katrina, she's right here. What! No! Oh my god."

D'neen hung up the phone and looked out of her window with a vacant stare.

"I don't know what to say," D'neen said in a weak

voice with tears streaming down her cheeks.

Katrina started the ignition and sped off.

"Where are you going?"

Katrina didn't respond. From the series of turns Katrina made, D'neen knew Katrina was headed home. Five minutes later the minivan came to a screeching halt in front of Katrina's door. Katrina hopped out the minivan and ran into her house. Charles was standing in his doorway watching the speeding minivan when it pulled up. D'neen exited the minivan and ran over to Charles.

"I need your keys," D'neen said.

"Where is your car?"

"I can't explain right now but I need your keys, it's an emergency."

Charles looked in his wife's tear filled eyes then walked in the house, D'neen followed.

Katrina ran to the basement. She was flabbergasted when she reached for the gun and it wasn't there.

"Lewis!" Katrina screamed.

Katrina ran up the stairs yelling Lewis' name. She raced into the bedroom. She stood there a moment discombobulated, then dropped to her knees crying. After a moment of sobbing, she opened the closet door and removed a box of baby clothes. She spread the clothes out on the bed. She then moved to the dresser and removed an envelope filled with ultrasound photos, taken when she was four months pregnant. She placed the photos next to the baby clothes.

"I'm sorry baby, mommy couldn't protect you. I'm sorry," Katrina said, her voice fluttering.

Katrina had a flashback to five years earlier, when she walked in on Ashley and Lewis having intercourse. Katrina had run home broken hearted, collapsing on the floor holding her stomach in pain. Lewis rushed in behind her, Katrina cried, something was wrong with the baby.

"Katrina!" Lewis said as he entered the bedroom

breaking Katrina's flashback. Lewis saw the clothes and ultra sound photos on the bed and shook his head pitifully at Katrina.

"Katrina, you have to get over this."

"If you didn't fuck that bitch I wouldn't have had a miscarriage, y'all killed my baby."

Katrina marched over to Lewis and poked him in his chest.

"Where is my gun?"

"I got rid of it."

Katrina slapped Lewis hard across his face and hit him on his chest with her fist screaming profanities at him. Lewis pushed Katrina on the floor.

"Calm the fuck down!"

"You better give me my gun!"

Lewis was unmoved. Katrina ran over to the bed and pulled the butcher's knife from under her pillow. She walked slowly towards Lewis who was scared, but he didn't let it show.

"Are you going to kill me Katrina?"

"Give me my gun?"

Katrina pointed the knife at Lewis' heart. He hesitated a moment, then removed the gun from his pocket and tossed it on the bed. As Katrina retrieved it, Lewis tossed the bullets on the floor, some rolled underneath the bed. Katrina snatched up one bullet. She was about to grab another one, but figured one was enough.

Across the street, D'neen stared into Charles' eyes and held his hand in her own.

"It's better that you don't know what's going on? Please, I need to borrow your car."

Charles handed D'neen the keys, she gave him a peck on his lips.

"I also need a wrench."

Charles looked questionably at D'neen, "It's a tool box in my trunk."

D'neen darted out the house. She looked relieved when she saw the minivan still parked outside. She ran back into the house, grabbed a knife from the kitchen, ran outside, and slashed the tires on the minivan. She then hopped in Charles' car and headed to the cabin.

Katrina walked passed Lewis while glaring at him. She exited the house, jogged over to the minivan, and was pissed to see the tires slashed. Katrina cursed D'neen.

D'neen pulled to a stop in front of the cabin and ran inside, startling Ashley.

"I have to take the bolts out from the wall."

"Why didn't you get a bolt cutter?"

"I didn't have time."

"Where is Katrina and Tasha?"

D'neen didn't respond. She grunted as she removed the first bolt. When she got to the last bolt, Katrina entered wielding the gun. Ashley froze in fear. D'neen, also in fear, stood slowly.

"D'neen, you betrayed me," Katrina said training the gun at D'neen.

"Katrina, I'm sorry but we have to end this."

"This ends when I end it."

Katrina wished she had grabbed two bullets, although she didn't really want to shoot D'neen. She then pointed the gun at Ashley.

"Please Katrina, please…Whatever I done, I'm sorry. This is going too far. I won't go to the police, I swear."

"Was you sorry when I lost my baby?"

D'neen and Ashley both looked shocked. For the first time D'neen realized that it had not been anger in Katrina's eyes, but grief.

"Katrina, what baby are you talking about?" Ashley asked.

"I was pregnant when I caught you and Lewis together the second time. That same night I miscarried."

Ashley finally realized the source of Katrina's hatred

for her.

"I didn't know you were pregnant, I'm sorry."

"You killed my baby and Tasha."

Ashley looked shocked, "Tasha is dead --I couldn't have killed her, I was here locked up."

"Because of your actions, my friend is dead. Now you must suffer the same fate."

"Katrina, taking a life is not going to make things right," D'neen said inching closer to Katrina.

Katrina didn't hear Ashley or D'neen as they continued to plea. Katrina carefully aimed the gun at Ashley, whose heart was beating wildly. Katrina squinted her eyes. D'neen could see that Katrina was ready to pull the trigger.

A second before Katrina pulled the trigger, D'neen threw the wrench at Katrina and hit her in the chest.

"Aaah!" Katrina yelled as she squeezed the trigger.

"Aaaaah!" Ashley screamed in pain as the bullet tore into her body, burning her flesh.

CHAPTER 41

FOUR YEARS LATER

A car with tinted windows drove slowly down Kelly Street. The block hadn't changed much besides the "For Sale" sign in front of Ashley's house, and a family of four exiting the house that once belonged to Katrina and Lewis.

The car stopped in front of D'neen's house. A visibly pregnant D'neen was walking towards her front door, at her side was her three year old daughter. D'neen had a sense that she was being watched. She stopped, turned around, and stared at the car questionably.

Katrina exited the car wearing a scarf and sunglasses. Although Katrina appeared to be incognito, D'neen recognized her immediately and looked a bit surprised. Katrina walked over to D'neen, who didn't look particularly happy to see her.

"Hello D'neen…This must be your little girl. She looks exactly like Charles."

"Go in the house baby with your father," D'neen ordered her daughter.

D'neen's daughter waved goodbye to Katrina then skipped up to the front door disappearing into the house.

"What are you doing here?"

"How have you been?"

"I'm good."

"How many months are you?"

"Does it matter?"

"It's good to see you and Charles are still together."

"He knows about everything, he's a forgiving man."

"His kind is becoming extinct."

There was a moment of silence, each woman searched for something to say.

"I didn't see you at Tasha's funeral," D'neen said.

"I couldn't come."

"Do you know that Bruce was murdered a week after the funeral…The newspaper said it was a robbery," D'neen said studying Katrina eyes for a reaction.

Katrina didn't flinch as she thought back to the day Bruce was murdered: It was a rainy Thursday night. The street was empty. Bruce was walking down the block, he turned the corner bumping into Katrina who was waiting for him. She was clad in a black rain coat and wearing a black baseball cap pulled down over her face. As Bruce apologized for the collision, Katrina, who he didn't recognize, stuck the knife in his stomach.

While Bruce laid on the wet ground dying Katrina turned his pockets inside out taking his watch and money, leaving the appearance of a robbery. The last thing Bruce heard was Katrina's voice whispering in his ear, "This is for Tasha." Bruce thought he recognized the voice before he passed away.

As D'neen watch Katrina reminisce, she had no doubts that Katrina was somehow involved in Bruce's murder.

"It's a shame what happened to Bruce," Katrina said.

"Yes it is --The police aren't looking for you as far as I know, for anything that happened four years ago," D'neen said signifying.

"I don't worry about the police," responded Katrina, understanding what D'neen was suggesting.

"I never thought you did."

"Tasha's daughter is getting big."

"I know. I take my daughter by to see her often,

they're friends."

"Like we were."

"It was nice to see you. I have to go. Take care of yourself Katrina," D'neen said turning away from Katrina.

"D'neen wait, take my number."

Katrina extended her arm towards D'neen holding a piece of paper with her number written on it.

D'neen was ready to respond, but held her tongue because she didn't want to talk with Katrina longer than she had to. D'neen took Katrina's number then walked into her house without looking back at her. Katrina walked briskly to her car, hopped inside, and drove away. As Katrina turned the corner of Kelly Street, she turned the radio on and heard a familiar voice.

"I don't do that anymore." Ashley said over the radio.

"Ashley, why don't you do shows like you used to? Everyone loved that stuff," The female caller said.

"You wouldn't believe how many people were affected by those shows. I turned over a new leaf."

"What made you change your format?"

"I not only changed my show's format, I also changed my life. And you can read about it in my book 'I'll Take Your Man', but I'll give you a taste…I had a cancer scare which turned out to be nothing. On top of that I was shot in the shoulder. I also had some interesting tattoos that I had to get removed. But the main reason for my change was my daughter Lou Lou. She's named after her father Lewis, he's a terrific father."

"Who shot you Ashley?"

"I don't know? Read the book."

"Come on, you know who shot you."

"If I did, I won't tell, I'm not a snitch."

"But you have it in your book."

"I'll never testify in court to anything in my book."

Katrina turned off her radio as she pulled into the radio station parking lot. She parked her car and removed the handgun from under her seat and laid it on her lap. She covered the gun with a newspaper, and waited.

Ashley exited her studio. Her attire and overall appearance was far more conservative than four years earlier. She headed down the corridor smiling and speaking to everyone she passed. She exited the building walking out into the parking lot and headed towards her car.

Katrina spotted Ashley from the other end of the parking lot. Katrina picked up the gun and opened her car door slowly. As she stepped her leg out the car, her cell phone rang. She was about to ignore the call, but something compelled her to answer.

"Hello?"

"Katrina, it's me," D'neen said.

"D'neen, it's not a good time."

"I just wanted to say, one of the strongest things a strong woman can do is forgive a person who hurt her."

Katrina held the phone for a moment speechless, affected by D'neen's words. Katrina hung up the phone and looked over to Ashley who was in her car rifling through the glove compartment.

Katrina closed her door back and weighed D'neen's statement. A moment later Katrina watched Ashley's car drive past her. Two minutes later Katrina placed the gun back under her seat, then pulled out of the parking lot and drove away.

THE END

COMING SOON

FROM

TA-LA-VUE PUBLISHING

"The Skilled Seducer"

By

Charlie Bassett Jr.

"Friends"

By

Charlie Bassett Jr.

♦TA-LA-VU PUBLISHING♦

To order a copy of "I'll Take Your Man" send a money order for $15.00 plus $3.00 for postage.

TA-LA-VUE Publishing
P.O. Box 942
Pottstown, PA 19464